HUNTED

A NOVEL

BOOKS BY JOHN HOLT

NONFICTION

Coyote Nowhere: In Search of America's Last Frontier

Montana Fly Fishing Guide—East

Montana Fly Fishing Guide—West

Knee Deep in Montana's Trout Streams, second edition

Kicking Up Trouble

Reel Deep in Montana's Rivers

Waist Deep in Montana's Lakes

River Journal: Madison River

All About Trout

FICTION

Guide Wars

Chasing Fish Tales

HUNTED

A NOVEL

JOHN HOLT

THE LYONS PRESS
Guilford, Connecticut
An imprint of The Globe Pequot Press

The Lyons Press is an imprint of the Globe Pequot Press.

Printed in the United States of America

10 9 8 7 6 5 4 3 2 1

Design by Nancy Freeborn

Library of Congress Cataloging-in-Publication Data

Holt, John, 1951-
  Hunted : a novel / John Holt.
     p. cm.
  ISBN 1-58574-780-7 (alk. paper)
  1. Corporations—Corrupt practices—Fiction. 2. Great
Plains—Fiction. 3. Supernatural—Fiction. 4. Greed—Fiction. I.
Title.
  PS3558.O3965H86 2003
  813'.54—dc21
                                        2003001229

FOR GINNY, JACK, AND RACHEL

ACKNOWLEDGMENTS

I would like to thank friends of mine who live the writing life—John Glisch, Bob Jones, David McCumber, Annie Proulx, and Danny O'Keefe. You get to the point where you ask, "Why the hell bother?" If you're fortunate, good friends, those who create because they have to, tell you in their various ways, "Because that's what we do," and that keeps things going for a while longer. Also, this is for Bob "I Left My Heart in Amarillo" Ray who taught me a bit about writing. Thanks to my editor Lilly Golden for her time and effort, which made this a much better book. And thanks to Mom.

Livingston, Montana
September 2002

When you give a hungry man a license

To do most whatever that he please

He'll lead you to the point of desperation

And then he'll want to drive you to your knees

"She Said 'Drive On, Driver'"
Danny O'Keefe

HUNTED

A NOVEL

O N E

The band of antelope stood on a rocky hill a couple of hundred
yards upwind of Joe Graves. The pronghorn does grazed on
the fresh grass that had burst through the moist ground of late
April. They would look up from their feeding, scan the horizon for any sign of danger, then drop their tan-and-white,
black-masked heads back down and resume eating. If alarmed,
they would disappear over the ridge in seconds. A big buck
lay just below the crest of the hill, soaking in the warmth of
the spring sun. His dark eyes looked down on his harem. *With
satisfaction,* thought Graves as he observed the animal through
the crosshairs of the rifle scope from his cover behind a clump
of scruffy junipers. The smell of the bushes reminded him of
gin, maybe with a splash of tonic, and he smiled at the inanity
of the thought. The 3x9 scope pulled the animal right up to
him. Graves watched as the buck blinked away mosquitoes
buzzing about his head and moist nose. *Sometimes I feel like
I'm being watched from behind through a rifle scope,* and he wondered where that thought came from, before pushing it from
his mind and zeroing in on a spot along the antelope's neck.
He sucked in a deep breath and squeezed the trigger. The

13

well-worn .243 issued a sharp crack. The buck's head jerked back, then forward. The animal rolled over and downhill before slamming against a rusty-red outcropping of clinker. It was dead. Graves never missed. By the time he lowered the rifle, a space of only a few seconds, the females were out of sight, long gone over the far ridge and probably hightailing it up brushy Mad Woman Gulch and then out onto the miles of tall grass, wide-open benchland that rolled off toward the Sanders Mountains, rising purple then late-winter-white over the border in Wyoming. Graves stood up, stretched, and side-hilled his way to the antelope. Blood oozed from a wound in the broken neck and soaked the grass, coloring both it and the salmon-tinted earth a moist brown. Graves grabbed the buck's horns and pulled the head down between his legs, then slit its throat to bleed the pronghorn.

He was almost out of meat. Only some mule deer pot roasts, a few pounds of catfish fillets, and a couple of rounds of smoked black bear sausage remained in the freezer and besides, he wanted fresh meat. He had a taste for it right now. He'd let the antelope hang and age for a while, but he'd fry up its liver in a cast-iron skillet tonight.

Graves had lived all his life in this harsh, dry country that lay well away from cities like Billings and Casper, land that had little to offer the well-moneyed tourists who were destroying the best of the West with their greed and rapacious self-absorption. Very little sparkling water for trout streams and no spectacular Rocky Mountain vistas or plush ski resorts to call in the babbling hordes of overdressed California or East Coast yuppies burdened with cell phones and an insatiable lust for money. Just dry, dusty expanses of coulees and bluffs, brutally cold in winter and oven-hot in summer, unspoiled country full of snakes, sage, cactus, poisonous spiders, flies, ticks, topped by never-ending skies filled with riotous amalgamations of clouds, stars, meteors, northern lights, and a whole bunch of stuff he never even tried to explain to himself or anybody else. More than forty years ago Graves had been born prematurely in the back of a banged-up black 1948 Ford pickup as his dad frantically drove on bald tires along narrow dirt two-tracks, sliding in the thick Workman Plateau dust, or banking off slight berms of soil and rock along the sides of the road, or flying through the air as the old truck leapt over frost-heaved bulges along the way and then came crashing back to earth in a wrenching cacophony of stressed metal. Graves's mother lay on dirty mounds of hay left from feeding their few cattle earlier in the day, her screams, as she pushed the child from her womb through the torn opening between her legs and out onto the now bloody hay, ripping through the pines and slicing across the clear air of the northern high plains. By the time they'd reached the hospital in Drew, a two-hour run, Graves was already wrapped in an old Hudson's Bay blanket, clutched in his mother's arms and suckling hungrily on one of her breasts. That's how Graves came into this life, and the rest of his years had been pretty much as free-form and unpredictable.

* * *

The thought of waiting until the autumn hunting season hadn't registered in his mind. No one around here worried about hunting regulations. He never had nor had his father or grandfather. Certainly not his great-grandfather who home-steaded this windswept, undisciplined country more than a hundred years ago, back when not many people came this way and even fewer stayed around. When they needed meat they went out and shot it. There was plenty of game in this country if you knew where to look and how to move with the land and within its subtle rhythms of coulee, bluff, cliff, hill, wind, and water. Antelope, mule deer, whitetail, even the occasional Roosevelt elk and black bear roamed the land, as did large num-bers of sage and sharp-tailed grouse, and Merriam's turkeys.

Only this morning Graves had killed one of the big birds, a twenty-five-pounder with nearly a foot-long dirty black beard growing out of its chest—a sure indication of an old turkey. He'd shot it in the head with his Savage .22-20 gauge after it first dropped down from its roost tree, a huge ponderosa pine that had been hammered by lightning strikes more times than he could remember, the tree's top a cluster of shattered, blasted limbs.

This country was dominated by open stands of the massive trees. The long, dead, brown needles carpeted the ground. Even the merest touch of breeze set up a lonesome moan through the big pines' branches. Large, sharp-edged cones lay in piles be-neath them. Graves had spent many nights sitting around warm fires tossing in hundreds of them one after another, watching as they burst into flame, the red and orange sparks exploding up into the night and sailing away, winking out one by one, sometimes many feet from the fire.

Twenty, maybe thirty of the birds slept in the battered ponderosa. As the dawn light came on over the country, the purest of light blues shading into the star-filled purple-black of retreating night, he'd watched as the turkeys awoke, dropped to the ground, and then clumsily shook themselves to organize their feathers. He picked out a large male from among the smaller jakes. The big boy was kicking up grass and dirt with his feet. He constantly shook his thick feathers and stretched and waggled his ungainly neck, the ugly red wattles making a queer sight. *Almost obscene,* thought Graves. He chose the older bird with its tougher meat because his woman friend was always impressed with how tender the flesh was when he finished cooking it. She always said, "Joe, this is so damn good. I love the way you do meat." She always said this and he always liked hearing it. When he shot the turkey through the head, the others went running off, putting and clucking in a terrible racket. They could move as fast as racehorses and were gone by the time he crawled out of his hiding place amid a pell-mell pile of crumbling sandstone.

The horizon had glowed silver at the approach of the sun. A lone coyote howled from a bluff a mile south. Then a band to the east picked up the riff and added a note of its own at the end, the animals' chattering and howling rising in pitch right to the end of the measure. The last cry reminded him of something Ornette Coleman had written—"Lonely Woman." A measure played in his head. The lone coyote seemed to pick up on the tune, extending the music and leaving it open-ended for the others, which took off from there. This went on with serious, new-day enthusiasm for a few minutes, and by the time the coyotes finished they had a pretty good little jazz melody going. *Better than Coleman himself,* thought Graves. He liked the way the coyotes talked. They sounded like the land looked to him. Free. Lonesome. Lawless. Hunting out here alone, this was how he lived. Where he lived. What he lived for. This morning he'd risen in the dark, dropped down a dry wash of limestone that lay before him like giant stairs leading to some ancient and now vanished monument. Then he'd scrambled up the side of a slope of loose yellow and gray rock, climbed across a thick seam of exposed coal before moving silently among the substantial, dark shapes of the ponderosas that rose silently skyward, and walked to his hiding place, where he pushed back in against the cold rock then waited to kill the turkey.

The bird's carcass was now hanging, nailed by the feet, to the shed behind his place. A couple of days of aging plus another marinating in a mixture of orange, pineapple, and apple juice along with Worcestershire sauce, freshly ground black pepper, and garlic. Then he'd call Mickey and ask her over for dinner. She liked the way he grilled the turkeys over white-hot coals with a closed lid for an hour or so. When the bird was cooked, its skin fired a rich brown, Graves would lift it from the grill, drop the browned flesh on a large wooden cutting board, slice the meat into large, juicy chunks, and bring it to the round oak table near the woodstove in his kitchen. They'd eat like wolves, ripping and tearing at the meat, and they'd devour huge Idaho bakers buried in butter and sour cream. Gnawed bones lay scattered everywhere and grease and meat juices ran down their chins and forearms. And they'd knock down a couple of bottles of red wine, maybe some California Merlot if that's what turned Mickey on that night, or maybe they'd work on a bottle of Jim Beam poured over ice in big glass tumblers. He preferred the whiskey, but he also liked to get laid, so if Mickey wanted the wine, he gave her what she wanted. He'd picked up a number of cases of the Merlot from a tiny winery in the Sonoma Valley three years before while back there visiting a gunsmith who did excellent work. The wine, the meat, the whiskey, all of it was a game and they both knew it. His submissiveness for hers later on. The ancient ritual gave them each pleasure. Once or twice a week this happened. Had been going on for years.

He cut off the antelope's head and gutted the animal. The blood on his hands and forearms dried quickly in the warm midday breeze. He wasn't interested in trophies to hang on the flat-cut log walls of his cabin or above the mantel of the fireplace. The horns on this buck were close to sixteen inches. Trophy horns by most standards. But he only wanted the meat. The remains fed the turkey vultures, ants, and coyotes. He lifted the carcass up and slung it over his shoulders. A hundred pounds at the most. Graves was just over six feet, weighed maybe 180, and could walk all day through this country. The two-mile carry to home was nothing. On the way back, as he skirted some more protrusions of clinker, he spotted a western terrestrial garter snake just before it slid into a dark crevice. The thing looked like a rattlesnake but was harmless. "Chickenshit," he said to the rocks and walked on. Back at the shed he strung the antelope by its hind legs with some soft hemp rope looped over a beam, looked across the miles of grass, sage, and blazes of wildflowers. He grinned at the insane beauty, then went inside to make some coffee.

A few days later, Joe and Mickey finished off the turkey, as always grilled perfectly, washed up, and headed out to the front porch for postprandial conversation. The night was early-spring warm, the air rich with the smell of new growth, of fresh grasses, the warming soil, and the budding leaves that were popping out on the bright, red-skinned alders, and willows that grew thick along a spring-fed creek bubbling away in a small cut in the hills nearby. Small brown trout, real small, darted about beneath the brushy overhangs and along the sandy streambed that was flecked with pieces of fossils he could never identify. The browns came from a hatchery up north. Mickey used to work as a fisheries biologist with the Montana Department of Fish, Wildlife and Parks, but ten years of bureaucratic nonsense, backstabbing, and career protecting at the expense of the fish and the rivers proved to be more than enough for her. Thoroughly outspoken during her tenure with the department, her determination to do what was right by the fish won her some admirers among her colleagues, and quite a few hard-core enemies. So when Joe mentioned the idea of stocking browns she called a friend at the Lewistown hatchery and was informed that the boys up that way were experimenting with a "hyper-strain" of browns from Scotland, one that readily adapted its growth and feeding habits to the size and food sources of a given stretch of water. After explaining what Joe had in mind, the biologist was more than happy to part with a few of his *"piscatorial wunderkinder."* She told Joe and he raced up there to pick up two hundred of the fry. So small they looked black like minnows. He'd hauled them back in a Coleman cooler and then dumped them in his place. Only a few had died from the trauma of the trip and the splashy introduction to his stream. The remainder had survived and grown in number over the years, spreading throughout the crooked miles of the creek all the way down to the main river. They never grew larger than seven or eight inches. Dark brown, covered in spots of jet black and flaming crimson with golden bellies. In fall the downsized males developed hooked lower jaws and humped backs, just like their much larger relatives swimming away in the state's famous trout streams. A couple of times each year he'd crawl on hands and knees up to the creek with a six-foot Tonkin cane fly rod his father had given him a long time ago and dap a small gray dry fly, nothing more than a wisp of elk hair, some gray dubbing, and a grizzly hackle. The tiny pattern would ride high in the current where it slipped under the willows or would spin around and around on the edges of bucket-sized eddies. The miniature browns would race out from the shade, slam the fly, and then race about in diminishing circles until he pulled the fish to him and shook them free of the hook. This brought him more pleasure than hunting the two-foot browns of the Yellowstone or Beaverhead. This world was everything a trout stream could be only condensed to a crystal-sharp intensity that thrilled him more than the raging pull of a five-pound trout ever did. The clear, cool water, the colorful rocks and sand, the protective cover of bush and grass, and those wild little brown trout. He couldn't explain the fascination and really never even tried to anymore. All he could ever say to Mickey was, "Damn yuppies won't float this baby," and she'd laugh.

They sat down in two weathered wicker chairs. Joe lit Mickey's cigarette for her and did the same for his large Honduran cigar. A bottle of Beam stood between them on a small table along with two glasses holding an inch or so of the amber whiskey. The heavens were turning on as darkness settled in. Jupiter was rising in the east looking like the landing lights of a 747, growing brighter as it climbed above the horizon. The sky still glowed a soft, deepening, and at once fading, orange far to the southwest over the dark shapes of the towering Sanders Mountains rising miles away in Wyoming. Above the porch hundreds of stars and distant galaxies dotted the sky. Soon there'd be thousands, then God only knew how many. Enough to make your eyes cross and your head spin. The land, the evening breeze, everything, hummed with the just barely subtle energy of spring exploding across the plateau. The northern high plains, country that looked so dead and lifeless in its dirty browns and dusty cover of old snow only a month ago, was coming alive in a hurry. Life flashed everywhere. Nighthawks boomed and hooted. Bats swooped right in front of their faces as the mammals fed on midges buzzing in the air. Kingbirds, meadowlarks, robins, swallows, and other small birds chirped and chattered in the dark. Glad to be alive and unable to contain themselves. The birds would go silent sometime after midnight and start all this again well before sunrise.

After working on his drink, Joe said, "We made it through another one, Mickey," and they clinked glasses and laughed at the absurdity of taking the wintertime struggle seriously and they shared a look, eyes sparkling in the night, a look about what had happened between them earlier that day alongside the dusty road that snaked through the emerald hills between her place and his.

Joe had just been returning from replacing a bearing on a windmill that provided water for the cattle out in a grassy flat a mile behind his house when Mickey pulled up. He'd also placed salt blocks for the cattle to lick in the stands of pines where they gathered to escape the midday sun. They decided to take a drive for no other reason than to enjoy the day and each other's company. They were driving down a road that wound between the pines and along the edge of a coulee, the truck kicking up red dust that the warm afternoon wind swept out over the vast sage flats. Rounding a ninety-degree turn, they pulled over next to an old grave that looked out upon far-ranging openness partially defined by a series of small valleys, nothing more really than eroded slices in the Workman Plateau. The cuts were filled with stands of ponderosa and juniper. A bunch of antelope jumped up from a near hillside and bounded away, rump hair flaring, down a narrow draw and away from view. The grave site was over fifty years old. On the tombstone was written APRIL 23, 1950—HERE LIES WIMPY QUINN. A GOOD, HONEST MAN AND MY FRIEND. THE DAMN BANK TOOK ALL HIS MONEY, SO HE DRANK HIMSELF TO DEATH. HIS ANGRY WIFE. The area was garishly decorated with clumps of plastic flowers—faded red roses; black-eyed Susans; purple, white, and orange tulips; and lots of carnations. Hundreds of empty whiskey bottles were piled in a mound along where Joe and Mickey imagined the body was buried. Four worn-out tires completed the arrangement, which was enclosed with four strands of rusted barbed wire nailed to gnarled pine stakes. Aluminum pie pans were hammered along the length of each post. An old fire pit surrounded by large stones was off to one side. Two rusted breaker bars lay in the middle, barely visible through the silvery-green sage now growing there.

Joe plucked a brace of cold Rainiers from a cooler in the bed of the truck and popped them both open with a whoosh and lots of foam.

"Ever know the Quinns?" asked Mickey as she took her beer from Joe and had a long drink. "Heard they had quite an operation during World War Two. A beef contract with the army or something."

"Dad was good friends with Wimp. Used to hunt and trap with him. Mink, otter, beaver, raccoon, jackrabbit, red fox. Even a couple of badgers. Some of the pelts are hanging on my bedroom wall. They helped each other out when one of them needed help, which, from what Dad said, was most all of the time for both of them," said Joe as he pulled two more beers from the ice. "Steers knocking down fences, irrigation ditches clogged, machinery broken down, pipes frozen, half the roof blown away in a winter gale. Quinns homesteaded 'bout the same time as my family. Before the turn of the century. Came out from southern Wisconsin same as we did. Irish. Whenever he talked about Wimp, and he loved the guy, he'd always end whatever story he was telling about the two of them together with 'Avoid the Irish,' and then he'd break up and actually roll on the floor with laughter. From what I heard, I could see why, but those stories aren't for the faint of heart."

"Joe, come on. Tell me some," Mickey pleaded. "Haven't I been nice to you lately," and she hugged him and pushed against him with her hips then moved quickly away with a charming *how-can-you-resist-this* smile.

"God, Mickey. You've got so many damn speeds I never know what's going on in your head. Maybe after dinner tonight." She grinned and held his gaze briefly before looking down at her feet. *She always gets her way,* Joe thought. She made him do things he would never think of doing. Like dancing or listening to classical music. Debussy over morning coffee. Waltzing on the porch at night. Joe kicked some dust into the breeze. And then he wondered and had to ask her.

"Are you seeing anyone else, Mickey? We've been doing whatever it is we're doing for a while, I just had to ask."

"Heavens no. Just keeping up with you keeps me occupied full time aside from my work." She sent him a demure smile. "If I were, I'd tell you. I promise."

And Joe said, "Okay." He believed her, but had lost his train of thought, and she picked up on that and prompted him.

"So tell me, what happened next with Quinn. Avoid the Irish and then what?"

"After the war the contract ended, and Wimp came up well short moneywise two years running. He'd expanded too much—new barn, too many cattle, new appliances for Adell. Wimp never saw the end of that fat run with the government coming. Dry years hammered his grass and that was that. Bank called in his loans. He would have been forced to move out, but instead decided to slam the booze. Must of smoked three hundred cigarettes a day, too."

Graves looked at several empty whiskey bottles of his own lying in the back of the old pickup. He pulled a gold-plated Zippo lighter from his pocket and bummed a Newport from Mickey. After lighting the smoke, he stared at the figure of a snake etched into the lighter's well-worn, soft finish. The reptile was a composite of square and triangular shapes with two mad oval eyes on top of its flat head and a grotesque curving tongue. His father, Joe Senior, or Señor as Wimp called him, had picked it up for a handful of ragged pesos while in Mexico City. Bought it from an old drunk who desperately needed a drink, a lot of drinks, while he and Wimp killed off a night hanging out in a dingy cantina thirty years ago; gave it to Joe on his twentieth birthday, saying "Light your cigs with this. You'll never quit until they pound the last nail into your coffin, anyway. Happy birthday." His dad was like that. Covering up his soft side with harsh talk. Senior and Wimp had driven down to Mexico in the old Ford truck loaded to the gills with camping gear and a few rifles. They'd read an account of the cats in an old copy of *Unknown Mexico* written by an anthropologist named Carl Lumholtz back around 1900. One year after reading the book the two headed down south of the border to hunt panthers in the rugged, untraveled Sierra Madre Occidental country, a land sparsely inhabited by Indians and cutthroat bandits. Far back in a deep, unknown canyon surrounded by sheer eight-thousand-foot rock walls, they came upon a band of Tarahumara, people who worshiped obscure gods with the aid of peyote, a reasonably strong hallucinogen. The Indians were open and friendly. The tribe asked the two with the simplest of sign gestures to join them for a feast that night, which included drinking a fermented tea made from the drug. While dancing and whirling around a fire, Joe Senior flashed the gold Zippo. A Tarahumara snatched it from him and disappeared. Wimp and Joe stayed up all night with the Indians. The next afternoon when Joe awoke, everything shimmering around the edges and looking a bit too real, he found the lighter sitting on top of his old Stetson. He noticed the engraving, the caricature of the snake sending shivers down his spine, and put it away in his pocket. The Tarahumara were gone. The village deserted, but both Joe and Wimp thought they could hear voices sounding like soft echoes floating around the place and drifting down from the canyon above them. Joe told his son that they'd followed the eerie voices that seemed to be calling them deeper and deeper into the surreal land for several days. They lived on enormous gold-colored trout, some more than thirty inches, that they snagged with a short casting rod, treble hooks, and lead weights they'd brought along. "Biggest damn trout I'd ever seen," said his father. Wading up the canyon through the middle of the cool stream, praying that it wouldn't rain and wash them away in a flash flood, they stumbled upon the tracks of an enormous panther. Tracks that pressed deep into the reddish sand. Four toes per print measuring eight inches front to back, the paired prints several feet apart and leading to a sheer wall. A few miles farther the voices were replaced with an unearthly howling that roared down at them and ricocheted off the sheer cliffs. The noise grew closer, deafening. Then the largest cat either of them had ever seen, an animal that dwarfed the 120-pound mountain lions of Montana, appeared on top of a large boulder, teeth glinting and deep tan fur shining in the orange light reflecting off the walls. The cat's yellow eyes were the size of plums. Later they estimated the panther at somewhere between 250 and 300 pounds. Both men raised their guns and prepared to shoot, but the cat crouched, leapt, and soared over their heads. They could smell its fetid breath, reeking of digesting flesh, as it sailed by. Before they could swing on the animal, it was gone.

That's all Joe's father ever told him of that trip, except to remark that those days in the canyon altered his way of looking at things. As for the lighter, he would only say when asked, "They must of known we have a lot of snakes up here in Montana." Following his return from Mexico, Joe Senior was taciturn where once he'd been almost ebullient. He still carried himself erectly but he appeared humbled, not proud to the point of arrogance as he'd been in the past. His mother, Elmer, and other area ranchers noticed the change, but as time passed they forgot the old Joe Senior and acted as though he'd always been this way. Joe put the lighter away, took a drag from the cigarette, and resumed his tale.

"Dad tried to help Adell, Wimp's wife, sober him up, but coming off the whiskey damn near killed him. Shakes. Convulsions. Hallucinating gigantic Angus bulls right in their kitchen stomping the old Monarch stove to pieces and punching holes through the floorboards. And so on. A real zoo filled with stuff that wasn't there. The second time, according to Dad, Wimp said 'Fuck this shit,' staggered out to the shed where he kept a stash of whiskey, and was dead in four days. Found him slumped over the wheel of his old Packard. Coroner said his heart gave out and his liver was close behind. Adell, Dad and Mom, just about everyone else around, buried Wimp right here. Took them half the day to dig through the rock and hard-packed dirt. Dad built the coffin out of cured slabs of ponderosa he was saving to make a dining room table. Lowered the casket into the hole with tow chains. Each person said a few words. Adell, smiling and crying at the same time, closed with 'I'll see you again, Wimp.' After the ceremony they drank themselves silly all night and most of the next day. Built a huge fire and roasted a couple of antelope over it. Right in that pit." Joe pointed a rough, tanned forefinger in the direction of the circle of rocks and then ran his hand through his thinning brown hair. "Elmer Yoter disappeared with his thirty-oh-six early in the proceedings and put the sneak on some does. There weren't nearly as many of them back then. They were bound for extinction until Teddy Roosevelt and others stepped in over the years. Elmer must of dragged the gutted animals for miles. No one at the wake heard the rifle shots. When he returned he was covered with blood, dirt, and prickly pear needles. In those days he was six-ten and weighed over three hundred pounds. He's shrunk some since."

"I just saw him driving around in that wreck of truck with all his dogs," Mickey said. "Barking and howling. What a racket."

"Yeah, he loves those ridiculous Boykin spaniels." Elmer, who owned a large ranch adjacent to Joe's, had bought four of them from a plantation owner in South Carolina and bred them himself. "Claims they're the best bird dogs he's ever seen. *Boykins.* Even the name makes me laugh," said Graves between sips of beer. "Curly brown nitwits. Make the springers I used to have look tame and they went wire-to-wire twenty-four hours a day."

"I meant Elmer." Mickey laughed and so did Joe. "Head out the window yodeling some crazed cowboy lament. Something about 'Cool clear water.' That mangy hat of his with the snakeskin band hanging on by a thread. Red-faced. Not something you see all the time and those dogs. Howling along with him."

"Always the four oldest dogs up front and the rest, eleven or twelve last I saw, howling and running around on the flatbed," Joe said. "Drives all day with them, rain or shine, summer or winter, drinking Pabst beer and Kessler whiskey. Fixed that muffler yet?"

"No. I could hear the damn thing coming for miles," she said. "And the clouds of exhaust. God, what a sight."

Elmer was at least eighty and never did like all the work involved with ranching, mending fence, repairing broken machinery, feeding cattle in the middle of a winter blizzard. But he got it all done just the same.

Joe bummed another cigarette from her. Inhaling, he paused then said through a cloud of smoke, "God, these things are awful," and Mickey laughed and told him to smoke his own. "I'm out. These will do. As for Elmer. He's got more money than the rest of us put together. He scored big on some oil leases recently, and sold the mineral rights to the coal under his land years ago. Dark Star Consortium owns the rights now and I heard talk in town the other day at The Mint that they're thinking of surveying the land in preparation for strip mining. And they're trying to revive plans to put a rail line along the Workman between Drew and Miles City. Anything to save a few bucks hauling the coal. Say good-bye to another chunk of this place . . . but . . ." Joe looked over a rise to the northeast and off into Dolphy River country. "They might want to get to the stuff soon. Some time ago lightning struck some exposed seams and that coal's been simmering away for years. The ground above is hot, even through my boots. On calm days you can see whiffs of smoke coming through cracks in the cooked soil. Looks like Yellowstone Park on his place, except without the water, or the tourists. Only things growing there are some scrub sage, withered cactus, and thistle. Cattle won't touch those sections. Neither will the game. February snow won't even stick to it."

"Do you still have those rights to your land, Joe?" Mickey asked.

"Yeah. I'll never part with those. What's beneath the grass is all part of it.

"Hell, at any rate, by the time they'd cleaned and skinned the does and stuck them on a couple of breaker bars over the fire, old Elmer was pretty well shit-hammered, dancing around while Coaker Triplett played the "Garryowen," Custer's marching song, on his fiddle. Man's still good. Puts Vassar Clements to shame. Elmer started leaping over the edge of the coals and eventually fell in. Dad and Coaker rolled him out of there and

Elmer was fine. Wool shirt was singed a bit, though. Hung it on a wall near his fireplace and it's still there. Goofy bastard." Joe looked over by the grave site to the fire pit and imagined he could see Elmer lying smoldering in the fire beneath the roasting antelope, juice from the cooking meat dripping on him and splattering on the white-hot coals, imagined he could hear the shrill notes of Coaker's fiddle, and imagined he could see his parents and their friends dancing around the blaze in the middle of that late-April night so many years ago. He turned away. "The rest of the wake was more of the same—drinking, dancing, bullshitting, and a little romance off in the dark. Sounds like a great time all things considered.

"The tires are from Wimp's Packard. Dad and a couple of friends pulled them off before they'd let the bank's repo man haul the car away. Shotguns and tire wrenches work every time. Wimp used to hunt out of that car. Threw the dead animals in the backseat. Dried blood all over the carpet and seats. Dog and deer hair as thick as a rug. Quite a rig. He'd cut a hole in the roof over the front seat. Used a hammer, file, and hacksaw, then rigged a canvas tarp over it. Probably the first sunroof in Montana." He smiled at the vision. "They never had any kids. Ran the whole damn place themselves. So after the wake Adell moved back to Clinton, Wisconsin, and lived with her brother's family on a dairy farm out there. She came back about twenty years ago. Stayed at my place for a few days. That's when she added the flowers and pie plates for what reason no one knows, and that's it."

"Life can be tough here, can't it, Joe. The work, the weather, and the drinking," said Mickey. Her eyes wandered out over the land. "Keep things small like you do and live modest. The hell with lots of money. Screw it. Right, Joe? Seems to work for you."

He looked hard at her and she returned the stare. *Screw it,* she had said, reading his mind again. *No peace in the valley for this boy,* he thought.

"Hundred damn cows, give or take, brings in enough for fuel, food, utilities, odds and ends. Place is paid for and I don't need much in the way of things. I've got all I want." His gaze followed Mickey's line of sight. *This country is plenty. All I could hope for,* he thought.

Before he could say it, Mickey turned to him and blurted, "And of course there's that outrageous blue-ribbon trout stream of yours," and that was it. They fell into each other's arms, laughing something about Mackenzie drift boats and Spey rods.

Then they began to kiss, passionately, fondling each other, but Joe pulled away and looked around for any approaching vehicles. Some of the roads went for days without use, and then it was usually a rancher headed into town or off to visit a neighbor; or there were the black trucks of the coal company's survey crews, side panels emblazoned DARK STAR CONSORTIUM, VEHICLE ID #1666 or whatever.

"Not here, Mickey. Anyone could drive by."

"Why not?" she asked as she dropped to her knees and worked on his belt and zipper. "Now, not later."

"No, Mickey. Not now." He made a weak attempt at stepping back, but she persisted, hands everywhere.

Joe gave in to another of his hungers. He never could control or resist any of them for very long—sex, hunting, lots of good food, whiskey. He leaned back on the truck's tailgate, looked down at Mickey, pushed his hands into her hair, and pulled her head to him. He looked off toward the Sanders Mountains, then he didn't see anything.

By then Mickey had Joe's jeans down around his ankles and had shed her cowboy boots and Levis. She pushed up against him and guided him in with her hands. Both of them were rocking and moaning, lost to the world, when out of the blue in a cloud of exhaust and thick dust Elmer and his pack of disturbed Boykins roared around the corner and into view, the old man's flushed red face, topped by that filthy hat, leaning far out the window, large mouth filled with stained teeth, lips flapping away.

"I'm an old cowhand from the Rio Grande . . . " Elmer's voice screeched and hacked above the roar of the mufflerless engine, sixteen spaniels howling and yapping along to the tune. Thirty-four eyes, some of them not yellowed and bloodshot, took in the action with carefree, maniacal delight. Seventeen tongues drooled in the wind. Joe and Mickey looked up from what they were doing, up at the insane sight of Elmer and all those dogs.

Elmer and his crew never missed a beat or an awkward note. Thundering past the two lovemakers, the dogs wagged their tails. Elmer tipped his hat, smiled, and tossed a full can of Pabst in their direction. The beer exploded on impact and rolled to their feet, shooting its foamy contents all over them. By then the chartreuse GMC flatbed was out of sight, backfires, awful singing, and godawful yowling trailing in a wake behind the menagerie.

Joe looked down at their soaked feet and ankles and said, "At least something came. I sure as hell can't now. Probably never will again." They looked up from the beer into each other's eyes and howled themselves. Bare-ass naked they hopped and leapt around the overgrown fire pit until Joe tripped over the pants around his boots and fell into the middle of it, pulling Mickey on top of him.

"God, we're as bad as Elmer was thirty years ago, but at least he had his pants on," said Mickey between spasms of laughter. "The more things change, the more they stay the same. Damn straight 'I'm an old cowhand from the Rio Grande,' " she sang. They rocked with laughter once again.

On the other side of the road a rattlesnake had been coiled on a flat piece of stone, nervously swinging its head about. Energy rippled along its muscular length. It began forcing its head against a rough rock, breaking loose the layer of dead skin around its eyes. Then it loosened the skin from around its jaws. Kinking and writhing its body, the snake worked the skin past its thick midsection then pulled through the remaining part, turning the shed skin into an inside-out, translucent replica of itself. Its new, bright scales glistened in the sun and the rattler slid away in a sidewinding motion, its skin rasping across the rock. The snake vanished into the dark shelter of a pile of jumbled sandstone, to hide for a while until its exterior toughened some. The red-tailed hawk, uncommonly impassive throughout all of this uncommon behavior, lifted its wings, working them up and down with growing speed. The predator rose thirty feet above the road. Then it swooped down and snatched the shed skin in its talons and soared off on a late-afternoon thermal, riding the rising air up over the plateau toward the distant mountains.

Joe and Mickey saw none of this. They lay there together in each other's arms, eyes closed, beneath the hot sun for some time before getting up, pulling their pants on, and heading on up the road to Joe's place.

Joe poured some more whiskey in each of their glasses, took a long puff on his cigar, and looked over to Mickey. They both shook their heads. What could they say about any of it. The two of them bouncing away together, Elmer, the truck, all those dogs and the raucous can of beer. They looked off to the eastern horizon. Chet Baker's long-ago trumpet playing in Paris drifted out to them from the living room speakers, the horn player's subtle manipulation of scales and harmonies floating within measured rhythms.

The intense silver-white crescent of a new moon rose above the horizon, casting shadows that ran black down the coulees. Ponderosa and sage threw long silhouettes across the land. Strange rock formations shone like quicksilver. Several coyotes barked in the excitement of recognizing the new, yet familiar, arrival in their sky. Suddenly, infinitely louder, a deep howl, rising up from the depths of an animal neither of them had ever heard before, washed across the plateau and ripped through Joe and Mickey's insides. It sounded like a creature from another world and another time. It wasn't a coyote.

A pair of Dark Star trucks lurched over the rough ground on Elmer Yoter's ranch. The new rigs were painted glossy black with the company's logo, a bright yellow bolt of lightning along the doors, the words DARK STAR CONSORTIUM done in bright red beneath the yellow. The men in the trucks were out to begin surveying the land in preparation for strip mining the coal sometime the following year. Seismic studies of the fifty-odd sections of land holding the mineral had been completed two years back. The four Dark Star employees had detailed maps showing where the seams of coal were, how far beneath the surface, how thick the layers were. Exploratory drilling had indicated that it was anywhere from twelve to thirty-seven feet and close to the surface. They had other maps showing how deep the groundwater beneath the surface ran and where it pooled into a large underground lake. Potentially the low-sulfur bituminous reserves could exceed a billion tons, enough to power the country for years. Dark Star had already reaped hundreds of millions of dollars from its holdings a few miles to the west over by McCoy, but these were beginning to play out and the company was preparing for the future. Trains pulling miles of cars were loaded with the black rock each day. Then they would haul their loads off to electrical generation plants at places like Colstrip and Gillette, Wyoming. Power facilities with enormous appetites.

The mining left huge holes in the earth covering thousands of acres. All the reclamation effort and technology in the world could not put the land back together again. Topsoil, tons of fertilizer, and oceans of piped-in water temporarily turned some of the ravaged land into an artificially green oasis that looked more like a Palm Springs golf course than the high plains. The easily duped eastern media bought the con, flashed stories of how low-impact strip mining was these days, a sustainable and environmentally benign source of energy; and of course the antelope and deer and elk loved the verdant grasslands, not to mention the piles of grain the company dumped all over the plastic scene. The phony place was a veritable delicatessen for the game, but most locals refused to hunt there—"Like shooting deer at Disneyland." And once the company stopped spreading fertilizer and water on the soil, which they did as soon as the press lost interest in the story after about fifteen or twenty minutes, everything died, turned into a wasteland.

In the coming months the survey party would map out the coal seams and haul roads to the proposed rail line along the Workman River, which was expected to be ramrodded through the Montana legislature, a hodgepodge collection of mostly bought-off political hacks. The line would be completed in as little as twelve months of blasting, grading, and degradation to the river corridor. Spread some money, make some threats, a little blackmail, the usual stuff.

The two trucks slowed as the terrain grew still more severe and distorted. More than two thousand acres of earth was faded shades of ocher and vermilion, jagged, heaved into abrupt hillocks that were fractured and broken. The sky was a bleak, burning white. Even in spring this part of Yoter's ranch felt unnaturally hot. A surreal vision of unmoving turmoil. Small clumps of desiccated sage and withered cactus dotted the landscape. Scattered about were groups of barren ponderosas, thirty-, forty-foot skeletons of sun-bleached gray wood. Their scraggly limbs thrust out like the arms of monstrous skeletons. Some of the trees, roots burned or rotted, had fallen over and were lying on top of each other, trunks cracked, branches shattered. The juniper trees, thick and dark green with dusty-blue berries elsewhere on the plateau, were nothing but brittle sticks, emaciated to the point where the always-wind found nothing to play with. Even in a gale the lifeless forms scarcely moved. Dead gray four-foot-tall stands of Russian thistle shuddered in the breeze like detoxing drunks. Recent spring rains had drenched the area. Still, this land was parched, baked bone-dry. Everywhere the men looked, plumes of dirty white smoke issued from vents and narrow cracks in the land.

"Goddamn place looks like hell," said a surveyor in one rig. "How in the name of Jesus can we haul our equipment in here? The damn ground will collapse. And as soon as we open up the topsoil, the rush of oxygen will set some of these underground fires off like a bomb."

"Don't sweat it," said the driver, himself an engineer and geologist who'd worked this country for close to twenty years. "We'll pump enough water to put out Hiroshima. And the ground is hard enough to support our rigs. Held up okay when the test-drilling crews came out a while back."

"Great plan, if you had the water," muttered the other, who was new to this part of the country. Appalachian destruction had been his beat up until this month.

"We do." The driver pointed down Mad Woman Draw, a brushy defile that twisted and turned between Yoter's and Graves's places. "Owner of that land," he said, pointing toward Graves's property, "has a spring on his land that's fed by a fair-sized aquifer. We'll tap that aquifer and pipe the water over this way. Run the line along the haul road from here over along the creek and down to the Workman when the new rail line is completed."

"What if the rancher won't sell the water?" asked the engineer as he lit a cheap cigar, blowing smoke that washed across the dusty dashboard and up the windshield. "These crazy cowboys out here hang on to what they've got most of the time. Damn land means more than money. Even when they're dead broke and starving."

"Don't sweat it. The company always gets what it wants."

The two in the truck exchanged a knowing look. Property rights and lives meant nothing to companies like Dark Star when billions of dollars were at stake. The cost of a hit on a man these days was only a few grand. Life was cheap. Coal was worth more than people to Dark Star.

"All of this looks the same to me. One piece of dry, worthless dirt pretty much like the next. Why here and not over there?" said the man from Appalachia, pointing to a large sandstone cliff rising above a large, grassy bench in the distance.

The truck's driver looked at his companion. "Why in the hell do they send me these dumb shits from back East? You don't know squat about the West."

And they continued to bounce across the parched land that covered the Fort Union formation, a geological structure that consists of three main sections, the Tulluck, Lebo and Workman River. The coal in these parts is largely folded under layers of sandstone that formed when an ancient sea dried up millions of years ago, and it's mainly located a thousand feet or more below the surface. For now the company was taking the easy pickings near the top. The company was mining the thick seams of coal where they trended near the surface. Geologists had determined that there was more than fifty billion tons in the region. Dark Star had all the time in the world. It could afford to wait out the ranchers. To a company like Dark Star that is only interested in the revenue generated by the coal beneath the surface, the land's beauty, open space and history means nothing. Without the coal it would be worthless to them.

The surveyor looked out the window at the shriveled carcass of a mule deer, skin drawn tight across the ribs, stomach torn open.

The driver checked the side mirrors to see where the other truck was. He slammed on the brakes. Five hundred yards behind, the front end of the other black crew cab was axle-deep in the ground. Smoke was billowing all around the rig and the two occupants had begun spraying fire extinguishers over the hood. The two in the first truck leapt out and ran back to their coworkers but by the time they reached the foundered truck, the machine was ablaze, all four tires burning. Clouds of oily black smoke poured across the land. The four men backed away just before the burning truck's dual gas tanks exploded, sending pieces of truck skyward and rocketing along at ground level. A chunk of door whistled toward them like a missile, slicing the surveyor's legs cleanly just below the knees. The man tumbled backward screaming, blood spurting from the stumps. Then a large ripping noise, like something was savagely pulling the earth apart, hammered through the air.

The ground at their feet tore open. The whole place shook violently, heaving in all directions at once. The three who were not hurt instinctively fled for their lives, leaving their wounded coworker thrashing. They ran, stumbled, crawled through and over cactus and unyielding sage, getting back up and running from the expanding crack in the plateau, running until their lungs felt like they were going to explode. When they stopped, having outdistanced the tear in the cooked ground, they looked back. Geysers of smoke, flame, and sparks spewed into the air along a yawning quarter-mile-long gash. The roar of the released energy was deafening. Burning pieces of cactus and whole flaming sage plants shot hundreds of feet in the air before plummeting back to earth in a barrage of scorching stone and burning bushes. The mangled man and the remains of the incinerated truck were gone.

Thousands of feet overhead five turkey vultures soared casually on six-foot wingspans describing large, lazy circles above the smoldering countryside.

Elmer pulled in front of Joe's place a little past noon. Mickey had left early for a fisheries management symposium in Billings. Now that she no longer worked for the state, Mickey did private consulting for out-of-state landowners who wanted their own private stream or pond gamefish populations. The work paid quite well. The scintillating affair was titled "Nongamefish Introduction in State Waters—Can We Learn to Live with It?" When she'd told Joe this, he just looked at her and walked over to the stove to pour another cup of coffee. A few days had passed since they'd been surprised by Elmer and his Boykins.

Joe was replacing his tractor's driveshaft, which had cracked when he was pulling some old tree stumps from the hard ground the other day. The work was almost completed.

When he heard Elmer's truck coughing and farting its way up the road, he crawled from beneath the machine and stood, wiping the grease and blood from his skinned knuckles on his coveralls. Normally the old man's arrival was heralded by loud barking and howling from the dogs. Today they were strangely silent. The only sound was the noise of the truck. The four spaniels in the front were seated in an even row looking through the windshield. The twelve in the back were neatly arranged in two rows of six on each side of the flatbed.

"How they hangin', Joe old boy," Elmer yelled as he lurched down from the truck, missing the running board and nearly falling on his face before executing a nifty 360 degree recovery, Pabst in one hand, cigar in the other. Even at eighty he was big: six-eight, close to three hundred. Old, faded blue jeans cinched by a thick leather belt below his big belly. Scuffed black cowboy boots and a huge washed-out green T-shirt with a pack of Muriel cigars in the pocket. A pint of Kessler protruded from his hip pocket. Silver hair curled out beneath his old hat. "What's ya think of the damn dogs. Ever since they seen you and Mickey goin' at it they ain't been the same."

"Thank God for that," cracked Joe as he snared a can of beer that Elmer winged his way. A pair of magpies went from tree to tree squawking heatedly about something. "Sorry about all that. We kind of got carried away there, in the heat of the moment."

"Sorry, my ass," boomed the old man. "Haven't seen a look like that on a man's face since I watched myself bouncing beneath a whore over in Wallace, Idaho, fifty years ago. Had mirrors on the ceiling, the walls, everywhere. But back to my dogs. 'Bout five miles past your little go-round yesterday, they all went dumb on me. Haven't heard as much as a yip out of 'em since then. And this goddamn military-drill-team shit they're pulling now, well . . . well I feel like shipping the whole bunch of 'em back to that cracker in South Carolina. Maybe they stand for that nonsense down there, but not this boy. No sirree Bob. No way in hell."

Elmer sounded mad, but Joe could see the laughter dancing around the corners of his eyes. He watched as Elmer surveyed the troops. Not one of the Boykins so much as batted an eye, wagged a tail, shook a long matted ear, or licked a chop. Elmer looked the whole pile of them up and down for several minutes then turned to Joe with what seemed to resemble pride.

"Damn. Sure as hell never thought I'd live to see the day where this ragged-ass bunch of brown-haired mongrels shaped up like this." He belched, broke wind, and slurped his beer. "Most contrary bunch of hounds I ever laid eyes on. Look at 'em. Not one of their damn ears moves so much as an inch. Eyes don't even blink. Don't get me wrong here, I admire them Northern Cheyenne just as much as the next fella, but I'll be goddamned if I'll have my dogs acting like they're members of those Indians' Contrary Society. A warring group like the Red Shields or the Elks is one thing, but this contrary business is another. Watch this!"

Elmer walked over and launched a playful jab at one dog's chest. Nothing more than a tap, really, but the Boykin didn't bat an eye and the other fifteen sat like marble statues, staring off into distant space.

"They think I don't know what they're up to, but I do. Smart little shits. Figure humans can do any damn thing they please, so why can't they. Like, for instance, screwing by the side of a public road in plan view of decent folk such as myself." Elmer cast a stern eye in Joe's direction, who at this point broke up laughing, spraying beer all over Elmer. "While we're at this, goddamnit, you're no better than these worthless, tick-ridden dogs"—they remained lined up rock-still on the bed and in the truck. "They're trying to break my spirit. That's what they're doing. Figure they'll drive me nuts and I'll lose my marbles. Won't be able to keep up with them and then they'll be able to run the Sam hell all over the place." He paused before turning on his canine tribe and pointing a huge, crooked forefinger at them.

"Guess again you lame pieces of cow crap. I ain't breaking. So forget about it." He turned back to Joe, who was still laughing. "Fuck you, too, Joe. This is serious. Man's got to at least have the loyalty and respect of his dogs in this world or he's nothing. Worse than nothing. Hell, that's not why I'm here. Came over to tell ya what happened at my place yesterday just 'bout the time you and your lady friend were whooping it up."

Joe had known Elmer all his life, considered him one of his few friends. They helped each other out with the ranch work or a busted pickup whenever it was needed. The man could talk a blue streak for hours and today clearly was going to be no exception, but before Elmer could start up again, Joe squeezed in a few words of his own.

"I wondered about those two Dark Star helicopters hovering over by Mad Woman this morning. Things make a tremendous racket, don't they? Vibrated the coffee cups off the kitchen table. What'd you do, shoot one of their survey trucks, Elmer?"

"Didn't have to. Damn fools took care of that themselves without any help from me. Drove out there as pretty as you please without a care in the world"—he turned back to his dogs—"and they sure as hell did fine and damn-dandy without any help from you worthless beasts. God, look at 'em. Wish the hell they could hold a point like that when I'm out ground-sluicing some grouse."

"What the hell happened over there, anyway?" asked Joe, who was looking past his friend's shoulder at the motionless dogs. "One of them drive into the gulch?"

"Not at all. Coaker and those damn mastiffs of his stopped by to pick up some wire and stakes I had lying around the barn. He's got some crazy notion 'bout fencing his cows in that pasture behind that old pump house during calving season. Thinks he can avoid running way out back to one of his godforsaken fields in the dark to winch a reluctant calf from its mother with a come-along in the dead of night come next March. Told him those cows will be so perturbed at being corralled, they're liable to miscarry, but the old fool won't listen.

"Anyway, seemed to get sidetracked here, Coaker does that to me. Those coal seams been burning since as long as I can remember and one of Dark Star's rigs broke through that hardpan. Thin as piecrust in spots. Should of had a man out front checking the ground." Elmer pulled out the pint, drained a third of it, and passed it to Joe who took a healthy slash himself and handed the bottle back. "Truck started burning real good and that sucked air down onto the coal. Next thing you know, at least what they told me this morning 'cause I was over at Coaker's helping 'em fix that cheap-ass baler of his, the ground tore apart all to hell.

"Truck's tanks exploded. Piece of door cut a man's legs off and then sucked both the truck and that poor bastard into the hole. Dumb shits. I told 'em those sections out there weren't fit for humans, but did they listen to me? Now they're out a truck and an employee. Probably could give a shit 'bout the burned-up man, but they sure worked like hell pulling that truck out." Elmer spread his arms out, palms up as if in supplication: *Why must I suffer these fools brought my way?*

"Watched the whole thing through my spotting scope. Hooked onto the wreckage with a grappling hook or something and those 'copters pulled it through the crack. What's left of it anyways. Fires gone down some, just smoke mainly. Their pickup looks shot to hell. Burned to a crisp." Elmer took another pull on the whiskey and looked over his shoulder at the sixteen statues. "I tell you, Joe, I told them idiots that they'd never get to that coal. Whole place is weak as the walls on a doublewide. Their business, God love 'em. Lightning's been touching that stuff off forever. Can't be all that much of the coal left by now. That's why I sold it to 'em. Easy money and a good source of hot-shit amusement for me."

"Been burning ever since I've been around," added Joe. He looked along Mad Woman Gulch. "Guess I'm glad someone's making money off those bastards. I hate 'em."

"Hate's a powerful word, boy. Careful if I was you on using that so damn easily. No damn good can come of it."

"I do hate them, Elmer," said Joe, and his face grew dark. "Sons of bitches throw their money around and think they can rape the land. Yuppies and coal companies, don't know which is worse. The hell with all of them."

"Calm your ass down. No sense in gettin' a hard-on this early in the day, least not for a coal company." Elmer laughed and winked at Joe, who smiled and reached for the pint. The old man continued, "Only signs of life I ever saw on that worthless piece-of-shit, burned-out flat were dead ones. Over on the edges of the burning seams I seen bunches of shriveled-up rattlesnakes. Piles of 'em. Must of been drawn to the heat. Slimy-ass reptiles. Don't have a brain in their heads. If they do, can't be no bigger than a piece of buck-shot. Those snakes look like big ol' used condoms. Ugly sight. Just plain ugly."

"Lovely image there, Elmer."

"And I've seen some kind of dog tracks," Elmer went on. "Big suckers, too. Maybe six, seven inches across. Shit, maybe more. Deep claw marks to 'em. Probably one of Coaker's mastiffs out scavenging those dead snakes. Saw 'em chomping away on an old tractor tire once. Be scared shitless to fall asleep around 'em. Probably chew my legs off or worse if you get my drift. Kee-rist those things are big. Little rain on the paw prints and they wash out to the size of a man-eating buffalo wolf. I saw one of those three-hundred-pound buggers when I was a boy." He killed off the pint. "Coaker's dad trapped it using a dead steer for bait. Must of been three, four feet at the shoulder. Teeth like spikes. Mean lookin' piece of dog. Haven't seen one since and I'm damn glad they're gone."

"Sure do get your share of lightning bolts over there, don't you Elmer?" said Joe. "Haven't had a strike here in years. Last one nailed that old tree behind the pump house and that's been it. Been a while."

"You're a blessed man, Joe. Truly blessed." The old man leaned toward Joe and winked. "Know what I mean? Don't suppose any of those fires are anything more than accidental do you? Just God's work. My hands are clean, so is my damn conscience for a change." He turned to the truck and yelled, "Cut the shit, damnit. Enough is enough, you lame-brained mongrels. Knock it off." Turning back to Joe with another wink, he said, "They think they're gettin' to me. No damn way I'll let those weasel-dicked fleabags get under my skin." With that he climbed back into the ugly-green truck. Then he leaned his head out of the pickup. "Listen up here a minute. Pay attention, damnit. If I were you, Joe old boy, I'd check into my holdings. Ya know what I'm getting at. Oil and that goddamn coal. Be nice to know what you own and what you don't. And that water of yours may be worth a pretty damn penny to Dark Star, too." He didn't wink this time. "Remember one more thing, and I don't part with this shit for just anyone. They can come and they can go." He looked straight into Joe's eyes, then fired up the truck. The engine caught with a loud catarrhal roar and the bunch of them, man and silent dogs, hightailed it down the road. The Boykins swayed some with the liftoff, but other than that they didn't move.

Joe watched them leave, watched the dust settle in the stillness, and thought for a long time about what Elmer had said. Those fires. Did he set them? Could he be that crazy, or that smart? Elmer had always been pretty short with his advice. Joe figured he'd better pay attention and check into a few things, like his mineral rights.

While Joe considered Elmer's warnings, the old guy barreled along an open stretch of road at nearly fifty miles an hour. The gravel and dirt lane ran across a vast, treeless sage flat.

Five antelope zipped into view, rising fast up out of a brushy draw. They ran alongside the truck for miles, keeping Elmer and the dogs company, all of them as wild as the Workman Plateau itself.

TWO

Two days after the loss of the man and the truck over on Yoter's property, six men sat in an office at Dark Star's holdings near the very small town of McCoy: nothing more than a post office/general store/gas station/second-floor residence and a whitewashed wooden flagpole displaying the country and state flags, both rectangles of cloth ragged around the edges from their constant flapping in the wind. The place was guarded by a graying yellow Lab, if by guarding was meant lifting his head an inch or two in semiconscious acknowledgment of the infrequent customer. That was McCoy.

The dead man's family in West Virginia had been notified by the operations manager the night of the incident, as the company was now referring to the tragedy. His mother had broken down and wept. The father had taken over the phone until he was told that there were no remains. Then a friend grabbed the receiver and finished up the gruesome call, barely. The charred wreckage that had been a pickup truck was lying in a heap in the gravel lot. All the men present at the meeting could see the mess. They only had to look out one of the wide windows. Of the men sitting around the maple table, three were the survivors. The operations manager, a geologist, and Bill Foxen—a corporate VP flown in last night by company jet from Denver—completed the meeting. A fax machine and several computers hummed along one wall. A coffee urn bubbled away on a stout table next to another wall.

The men discussed damage control in the media. The conversation was conducted by the operations manager and Bill Foxen with occasional nods and brief comments from the others. Given the somewhat bizarre nature of the death on Yoter's property, the story had gone national with aerial views of the disaster scene flashing across the airwaves. Dark Star had weathered much worse than this over the years— deadly cave-ins and explosions back East, ugly evictions of landowners in Utah, photos of the scars left from the strip mine in Montana running in a national magazine then picked up by the major wire services, the usual. They'd ride out this glitch in the proceedings until it faded from view, perhaps in a couple of weeks or so. The much larger issue was what to do about the coal the Consortium had paid good money for on Yoter's land.

After several hours of input from the other five, Foxen leaned back and lit a Cuban Flor de Cano cigar with a trio of stick matches. He held the flames from the first two matches just below the end of the cigar, rotating the thick Churchill between his thumb and forefinger slowly in the heat of the invisible upper end of the match flames until the tobacco began to smoke slightly. With the third match he put the cigar to his mouth and drew on it slowly. The tip flamed briefly then died down. The VP sucked in a large mouthful of smoke, savored the rich spicy taste, then exhaled through pursed lips a thick cloud of blue-gray smoke that partially obscured his face for a few seconds. He held the cigar out in front of him, admiring its even brown color and perfect, cylindrical shape. He smoked in silence for some time. Finally he leaned forward while exhaling a huge cloud of smoke.

"This comes down to the basics," he said in a lazy southern-Rockies voice. The VP was close to seventy but looked ten years younger. "Do we go after that coal or don't we? Do we write all this off as an operating loss or do we take the risk and go after that stuff out there?" He jerked a thumb over his shoulder in the direction of Yoter's place. "My decision is, and I have the authority to make it, my decision is we go after that coal. We do whatever it takes."

The operations manager nodded in agreement. The other four men were stunned. After all that had happened and the no doubt vastly diminished state of the reserves on Yoter's fifty-three sections, they figured that it was a foregone conclusion that Dark Star would back away. They were dead wrong.

"We have the capital right now. We're in good shape," the VP continued. "And we want to send a message not only to the industry, but also to the people living out here, that when we buy the rights to something, come hell or high water, we're damn well going to have our way.

"Even if we only pull out a third of what we originally estimated is buried over there, we'll show a small profit and make a big point," he said with a grin that was wrapped around the butt of his fat cigar. "This is how we'll proceed, and Pete, I'm counting on you to organize this action and, if necessary, ramrod it through to its conclusion."

Operations manager Pete Kilduff was a sandy-haired man of medium but wiry build in his middle forties. He nodded. He'd been in difficult spots like this before. Like the one down in Utah, and he loved not only the challenge but also the controversy and the energy that swirled around this type of mayhem.

"You got it, Mr. Foxen," Kilduff said in a deep Texas drawl. Kilduff and the VP were longtime friends, but Kilduff always called the man Mr. Foxen in front of the others. It helped to bring home in a subtle way that Dark Star functioned down through the chain of command, top to bottom, like the military. "My word on it."

"I already knew that, Pete." The two shared an inside smile born of playing hardball against all comers over the years. "I want that aquifer beneath Graves's place tapped and those coal fires put out. Start in on the water-rights negotiating and slam his ass with the fact that Daddy jerked him out of his mineral rights to pay off gambling debts and his drinking and whoring up in Billings years ago. Even back then a couple of hundred grand was cheap money considering all the coal out there. The old man had to be desperate to sell them and to keep it a secret all the way to his grave. While you're doing this, start drilling over in Mad Woman Gulch on Yoter's property. Angle in on Graves's water from the side. Near as I can figure from these maps it's only a seventeen-degree pitch—"

"Closer to fifteen, boss," said Kilduff as the other four men watched this whole unbelievable course of action unfold. They'd never been in this ballpark before and were at once frightened and excited. "I've already ordered the crew to ready the rig and bring up the new bits that came in from East Carbon. We should be set to go in a week at the most. We can skirt the burning turf and drive in over the draw just to the south. Sand wash on top but firm underneath. She'll hold our rigs. A little aggregate and some grading is all it'll take."

"Good man," said the VP as he worked on the cigar and doodled on a notepad. Just lines and vector arrows pointing in all directions drawn in blue ballpoint. "Any questions?"

"Just one," said Kilduff. "What's the budget on this one?"

"Sky's the limit," said the VP. "You've got my authorization with the boys in Denver." He stood up. "Any other questions?" There were none. "Good. I've got an appointment for dinner in an hour. Pete, call me in the morning before I head back to Denver."

Foxen mashed out his cigar in a coffee cup and strode out the door. The meeting was over.

★ ★ ★

He was in bed with two of them. Legs, arms, breasts, sweaty hair, lingerie, the whole works. Billings's whores. Fifty bucks apiece all night. Whiskey and gin bottles and glasses filled with the booze were scattered about the room. Ashtrays jammed with cigarette butts. He'd come up from his ranch on the Workman two nights before and had been gambling, drinking, and screwing ever since. For a change he hadn't lost a lot of money at cards. He had card sense, when he was reasonably sober, which wasn't most of the time up here. Normally on these three-day binges he would leave town a couple of grand lighter from the poker, and there was the whiskey and women. Not this time. He'd finished up last night a few hundred ahead. He'd been drunk when he engaged the hookers and the three of them had been at it all night. All sorts of convoluted positions and combinations and as this new day approached, the dawn light starting to show as a soft gray through the room's lone window, he was played out. He got up and drained a glass of last night's bourbon sitting on the dresser and then one filled with stale gin. He fought to keep the liquor down as it burned and boiled in his stomach. He told the two women to go back to sleep and left a pair of fifties on the bedside table for the ladies, dressed, walked out the door, quietly closing it behind, down the dingy hall and out onto the street to get some coffee and breakfast at a café around the corner.

The waitress brought coffee without asking and he ordered eggs easy over, hash browns, sausage, toast, and juice. *Takes stamina to keep this up,* he thought and laughed quietly.

Not a happy sound. He stirred three spoonfuls of sugar in the coffee and drained the cup in one take. The waitress had it refilled before he could look up to signal her that he needed more. Then she was gone. She'd seen his kind before. Men living out their private hells and warring with their demons. She left him alone.

Joe Graves, Sr. liked to think of himself as a good man, an honest one, but like most men he knew better. Getting through the day-to-day involved making choices and doing things he was, at best, uncomfortable with. His wasn't a glamorous existence. Cattle and lots of hard work, month after month in dry, harsh, relentless country. Didn't make much money at it, either. Life with his wife was a series of accommodations, acquiescence, and subtle humiliations. They hadn't had sex together in years, since shortly after their son was born. Before that she'd been extremely aggressive and adventuresome, showing him things about sex he'd never even thought of. And Kate dressed to please him. Wore her hair long the way he liked. Silky slips and panties. Garter belts and stockings. She kept him in a constant state of arousal. But since the birth of their son she had changed, cutting her hair short, wearing nothing but loose-fitting cotton dresses and, worst of all, hideous flannel nightgowns to bed. He felt like he was sleeping with his mother. So as far as their love life went, there was none. At first she'd stalled him, saying she needed to recover from the birth. By the time she had, the two of them had drifted apart, grown distant. They were no longer even friends, merely strangers sharing a home. He tried a few times to approach her, but she rebuffed his clumsy attempts. If he pressed the issue she would become angry and tell him that she no longer loved him. He turned, as most men of faithful intentions do under these circumstances, to masturbation, but this wore thin after a couple of years. Unfulfilling to the point of boredom, even depression. He resorted to drinking whiskey after he'd completed a day's work or occasionally playing cards with his friends.

Ten years ago on a trip to Billings, a greasy oil town with unrealistically big expectations, *Denver of the high plains* or some such drivel, while picking up some parts for his tractor along with a new hot-water heater, he made a decision. The bearings for the tractor didn't come into the parts store until after five, and the water heater wouldn't arrive at the appliance place until the next morning. He'd called his wife, explained the situation, said he'd get a room in town and be back by midafternoon at the latest and she sighed like he was the one responsible for the delays and hung up. Pissed off, he went to the nearest bar and poured down shots of whiskey, which he chased with schooners of Grain Belt beer. After eating a chicken-fried steak and a pile of mashed potatoes smothered with gravy and fried onions at the bar, he adjourned to the back room and its nonstop poker game. Ranchers in for the day, slickers, drifters with a few bucks in their pockets, local businessmen—there was always a game in the smoky, windowless back room. Sometimes for decent stakes. He played until past midnight and lost a little money.

Forty dollars. Then he pushed away from the table, bought a bottle of whiskey from over the bar, and walked out onto the dimly lit street and the drizzle. His room in an old derelict hotel was only a block away.

Before he'd gone twenty paces one of Billings's numerous hookers approached him and asked if he needed someone to share his bottle with. He'd never been unfaithful to his wife. Never even considered it, but without hesitation, without asking the cost, he said, "Sure. Why the hell not," and the two went off to his room with the lady draped around him. In the dingy room—single bed, gray linen, washstand, night table, no lamp, bare lightbulb overhead—the two smoked cigarettes and worked on the bottle. He poured out his miseries concerning his marriage. She was a good whore. She listened and touched his knee and then his thigh during particularly traumatic junctures in his narrative. Then she got up and took off her clothes and stood before him in the sheerest of white panties and bra. He instantly forgot about his problems and his excitement was clearly visible when the whore undid his zipper. In what seemed an instant to him, they were in bed and she had him inside her. After years without sex with a woman, the sensation of her rocking up and down while she straddled him, the warm moistness, was beyond memory, beyond anything he'd ever experienced. It had been that long. He squeezed her firm breasts in his hands, pinching her erect nipples, and arched up to get into her still farther. When he came, he groaned "Oh, Jesus!" and sank back into the bed. The whore wasted little time. She climbed off him, cleaned herself at the washstand, dressed, took a twenty from his wallet, bent over and kissed him on the forehead, and left the room. He was up for hours reliving the all-too-short experience, finally falling asleep near four A.M. A few hours later he awoke resolved to make this a regular part of his life. He'd done without the basic pleasures for far too long. The hell with his wife and her frigidity. He was a man. He was alive, goddamnit, and he smiled at this newfound vehemence and determination. He hopped in the pickup, picked up the tractor parts and the water heater, then drove home down along the badlands that pushed up to the Workman River. He sipped whiskey and beer on the way home, driving at a leisurely forty miles an hour on the oiled-dirt road. He was enjoying himself. His new, almost euphoric mood did not go unnoticed by Kate, and she pretty well figured out what had happened up in Billings. Their relationship moved from benign neglect to one of torment. She exacted her revenge in so many carefully thought-out, subtle ways, Joe thought he was going to kill her. She seemed to know his every move and his every thought. Everything in their marriage shifted slightly to keep him either off balance or angry or hurt. Objects around the house were ever so slightly moved. His eggs were just barely undercooked. His jeans were still neatly folded in his dresser, but damp. She made seemingly innocuous comments about how his hair looked or the state of his boots. And she would move his whiskey from cupboard to cupboard with no discernible pattern or rhythm. He'd spend long minutes looking for it until she would walk over to a certain shelf and grab the bottle with an angry flourish. He'd snatch it from her, stomp out onto the front porch, collapse into a wicker chair, and drink straight from the bottle, the bourbon tasting sharp and fiery in his mouth. He was being driven crazy and they both knew it. He was desperate. He needed to get back to the whiskey, the cards, and, most of all, the whores in Billings, but times were tough and he was short on cash for such doings.

As is so often the case, fortunately or unfortunately, depending on your perspective, the solution to this difficulty walked right up to him while he was in Drew running errands. He'd stopped at The Mint for a couple of quick ones and his life changed.

He knocked back his second shot of bar whiskey and took a sip of beer, lit a Pall Mall, then leaned his elbows on the scarred wooden bar and rested his unshaved chin on his fists. A couple of stools down, a man in crisp jeans and checked shirt with pearl-inlaid buttons, new straw hat pushed back on his head, was talking to the bartender in a medium-volume voice that had a suggestion of Texas in it, but not much of one. He was tanned and looked fit, hard and lean, probably in his late twenties.

"Tell ya the truth, Dutch," said the guy. "I miss the hustle and the A-Rabs over there in the Middle East. Crazy bastards drink their own piss to purify their bodies. And the way they treat their women—if we tried that here, we'd be castrated. But I don't miss all the heat and sand. Stuff got into everything. My eyes were always red and burning and my skin was rubbed raw before it turned rough like cheap leather. Mark my words"—he had a soft drawl—"someday them desert savages are going to be worth more money than anyone ever thought existed. It's that goddamn oil lying beneath all that sand. Those camel drivers are going to be filthy rich." He sipped from his drink.

"And when you look at it, this buying up the mineral rights around here is tedious, hell, make that downright boring, at times, but Northern High Plains is a good company to work for. Medical, decent pay and incentives, and plenty of time to myself. Just got the rights over on Vallie Eave's place up along Hayne's Coulee sewed up yesterday. Lots of coal on that land. Can see some of it along the edges of the land where it breaks off. Two hundred sections give or take for thirty an acre comes to close to four million and I make one-point-five percent on that or sixty thousand. Mind you, that's in addition to my salary. Three or four of those a year and I'm doing okay. More than okay." The man flashed a big grin that let Dutch know this was someone who was sure he had the world by the balls.

Graves leaned a bit the man's way, sipped his beer, and pointed to his shot glass and to the man's glass. Dutch filled them both and took a couple of bucks from the pile in front of Graves, who leaned over and introduced himself and asked what the deal was with the coal.

"Glad to meet ya, Joe." The man slid off his stool and walked over and shook hands with a firm grip. "Name's Bill Foxen. Work for Northern High Plains Coal out of Gillette. I've been buying the mineral rights from ranchers around here. Helping you folks out with a little cash you didn't expect to have. Mainly coal we're interested in. Nothing as big as what Dark Star is starting up by McCoy. We just want to get a foothold in this country. Sort of looking off in the future, you might say. Probably won't even consider working any of it till well into the next century if even then. Hell, we make money on taxes just by spending money." Bill drained his drink, nodded for a round for each of them, adding, "Pour a stiff one for yourself, Dutch," and turned back to Graves. "Beats me all to hell how a company can make dough by spending it, but that's the way she shakes out, at least so they tell me."

The answer to Graves's cash woes was right here if this man was interested. Over seven thousand acres at thirty per was more than two hundred thousand. Enough to pay off the last loan on his land and home, and more than enough to go up to Billings or, what the hell, even as far west as Butte, whenever he wanted. Man can raise all sorts of Cain in that town.

Graves and Bill discussed the eleven sections, where the land was located, and if he had clear title to it. Bill told him he'd meet Graves out by the road that dropped down into Mad Woman Gulch at seven the next morning. Kate was up in Great Falls visiting one of her friends for the next week and maybe he could sneak this deal through without her knowing.

They had a few more drinks. Graves let Bill in on a portion of his woes and the need to do the deal on the sly. Bill said "no problem" as long as the land was in Joe's name and Graves said he'd bring the papers, including the ones showing that he needed to pay off around thirty thousand to free up everything. The man from Northern High Plains was out to buy the rights to ranchers' coal, whatever it took. Going behind the back of this guy's wife was part of doing business, closing the deal. Bill said he had access to an attorney on a retainer for Northern High Plains who could draw up the agreement in such a way, it would take a sharp lawyer to figure out what had happened—that Joe had sold his mineral rights to someone else. Bill said he understood about women and how they wanted to run everything and poke their noses into "business that concerns only men." He'd take care of everything. The payment, if things panned out, would be "no problem," according to Bill. Eleven sections, while "a fair piece of land," in Bill's words, wouldn't "hardly put a dent in the company's acquisition fund." And Foxen was as good as his word. The coal on Graves's land was well below the surface, but the company figured in time the country's need for energy would drive the price of the stuff up to the point where digging down hundreds of feet would still turn a profit. According to current surveys the seams on Graves's land ran from twenty-three to thirty feet thick. He let Joe think that he'd driven a hard bargain, that he was a shrewd businessman-rancher, finally settling on thirty-three bucks an acre after initially offering twenty-eight.

Foxen had been prepared to go to forty and earned another little bonus for coming in under this figure. All told, figuring in taxes and legal fees, Graves walked away with close to two hundred thousand.

When Kate returned he told her he'd decided to pay off the bank by closing his savings account, which had about thirty-seven thousand in it. Before she could make a scene he showed her the clear titles to their property and home in both their names, and a term life insurance policy he took out on himself for half a million with her as the sole beneficiary paid up for ten years. He also gave her a thousand in cash that was left over, saying, "I just wanted you to feel secure in case anything happened to me," and she actually smiled a real smile and gave him a genuine hug. During this rare show of affection Joe was thinking *Damn you Kate, I've got enough money to do whatever I damn well please now,* and he smiled while hugging her.

Within a month the deal was done. Graves sat in his truck parked on the street outside the Northern High Plains office in Drew reading over all the legal documents, especially the title agreement and the language describing the fact that Northern High Plains Coal owned the mineral rights. His eyes crossed and his brain got fuzzy just trying to put the words together as he read the elaborate legal jargon. No way in hell could Kate figure out this lawyer bullshit.

The hell with her, he thought. *She loves the damn kid more than me. Hell, she only puts up with me because I have the strength to take her crap. I'm nothing but a punching bag to her. Fuck you*

Kate. I hate you. Can't believe I ever loved you. He didn't hate his son. He resented the kid and was jealous of all the affection his mother showered on Joe Jr. He promised himself he'd never let his son know how he really felt about either him or his mother. No good purpose served by that went his reasoning. *What a sick damn life I'm stuck in.* He took a deep swig from a pint of whiskey, then cleared his throat and spit out the truck's window. He fired up the aging pickup, drove out of town, turned onto the long road that climbed on top of Workman Plateau and led to the ranch. "The hell with all of them," he said out loud.

From the top of Chambers Point Joe Jr. could see for nearly seventy miles in any direction. The unspoiled bluff country of southeastern Montana stretched from horizon to horizon, thousands of square miles of ragged coulees, ponderosa pine forest, sagebrush and native grasslands. Infinite variations on shades of red, pink, orange, yellow, gray, green, blue. This was one of the least known parts of a little-known land. To reach where he was standing took three hours of lurching and crawling his old truck over rocky two-tracks that eventually faded away to nothing. Then a few more dusty, hot hours scrambling and crawling up steep cuts littered with broken rock. To reach the top, you paid with sweat, blood from skinned knuckles, palms, and knees, burning lungs, and cramping leg muscles as you clawed and pushed through the rubble to gain a thousand feet in elevation. The surrounding sea of hills and crumbling sandstone cliffs stood out in stark relief against a cloudless dome of sky. In extremely dry country this wasted piece of it was a desert. The place was without water. Storms would build in the west, enormous clouds billowing thousands of feet above black shrieking bases of roiling rain and hail. Bolts of lightning, cloud, and earth fought in electric violence. Rain fell in torrents as the heavy weather swept over the plains. Then the massive clouds would shrivel up and vanish like smoke in the wind before they deposited so much as a drop of rain around Chambers Point; or the rain would fall only to evaporate back into the sky, never reaching this forsaken rock and dirt. Even cactus was in short supply here, mostly pods of prickly pear that were shrunken, desiccated. Clumps of sere bluebunch wheatgrass clung to tan-colored soil baked as hard as concrete. Dry washes were worn smooth by the wind. There were no signs of fresh cutting from the rushing runoff of infrequent spring downpours common to the rest of the Workman Plateau. For some reason this outcrop repelled the rain—through some force pushing it away. So there wasn't any water here, except for a tiny spring near the summit of the point. A moist anomaly that somehow, by a curious construction in the layered rock, was forced upward in a meandering path until the water seeped out far above the plateau on this blasted point of nowhere. A miracle of sorts. A meager trickle of warm liquid that spread its life out in a small, irregular circle of olive-green moss and diminutive specimens of threadleaf phacelia, the plants' delicate pink flowers an incongruous sight, shining in the spring sunlight high up here in the midst of this pile of barren desolation and parched chaos. Even rattlesnakes were rare in the Chambers formation. Joe had spotted perhaps half a dozen in the thirty years he'd been struggling into this pocket of isolation where he'd never encountered another human soul, all the snakes not far from the water, sunning themselves on narrow ledges and not even bothering to rattle at his passing.

For some reason the biggest turkeys he'd ever seen hid out in this trackless mayhem. Unexplainable as was so much of what happened on the plateau. Here were ridges and belts of rock that looked like they'd been heaved up and then slammed around by an enormous being in some uncontrollable rage. Epochs of these striations sliced through one another without order. Precambrian sedimentary rock shoved between Tertiary gravels in diagonal thrusts. Mesozoic shale, limestone, and sandstone ran bright within this in horizontal bands of ocher, tan, and gray. Proterozoic, Pliocene, Triassic, all mixed together in a scene of such gigantic disorder, it was beyond comprehension. Why the turkeys picked this place was beyond Joe. He'd killed a thirty-two-pounder when he was in his teens, back when he'd first found this area by accident one day while roaming the backroads on his way from the bucking horse sale in Miles City. He was hooked as soon as he stepped out of the truck and looked up at Chambers Point. Again, he couldn't explain the fascination any more than he could his little stream and even smaller brown trout.

Some places called to him powerfully and he always answered, unable to resist the force of the land when it spoke to him. Two years ago he'd killed an even larger bird. There was little mast for the turkeys to feed on save for the bunchgrass. No ponderosa pinecones. No grain from ranchers' fields. Nothing. A few crickets and near-dead grasshoppers. And the only water was this little spring. Yet the large birds came to this microscopic oasis every day at sunset during late April. Joe wasn't interested in trophies, but fighting his way up here, hiding behind a pile of shattered sandstone downwind of the spring, and head-shooting one of these enormous turkeys was the flip side to the thrill he got fishing for his little brown trout back home.

He'd packed a bedroll, some food—nuts, dried fruit, jerky, a bottle of whiskey, water, some bandages and codeine-based painkillers in case he hurt himself. Nothing else save his rifle, pocketknife, and some matches. He liked to be out in this empty country with as little as possible, and what he brought was always enough. Hunched down against the rocks out of the wind at night sipping the whiskey and maybe even enjoying the sharp flickering of the smallest of twig fires, the wood scrounged on his way up, he felt free, unburdened from all the madness and anxiety down below. He was part of all this emptiness and he never felt more alive. Nothing compared to the time he spent on top of Chambers Point.

"Lived here all my life," he said to the wind. The sun was edging down toward the western horizon, deepening from blaze yellow to intense orange as it declined in the sky. "Sometimes the days last so long it seems like I've lived one life too many." He took a sip of water and ducked back down behind the rocks.

Earlier in the day he'd driven into town and dropped off title papers, sale agreements, and anything else related to his ownership of the ranch for his attorney to examine. The secretary took them with an outstretched hand and a plastic smile, saying that Kid would look them over and give him a call next week. Joe said that was fine, drove home, loaded the gear; now he was here. Something in Elmer's words had triggered a warning within him, and the state of affairs concerning the mineral rights bothered him. Coming to Chambers Point was a way of clearing his mind and catching his breath. He looked out over the country to the north. At night he could see the lights of Miles City, a real cow town dying an ugly death at the hands of developers. They had latched onto the town after a barrage of articles about the annual May bucking horse sale and all the "real West" goings-on. Now the south side of town was strip developed, littered with Kmarts, Wal-Marts, McDonald's, mini marts, the whole nine yards of junk and bargain-priced greed that eventually revealed its astronomical true price. And the streets and parking lots were filled with SUVs, BMWs, Hummers, and the like driven by Californians and East Coasters who'd accumulated tons of money doing nothing but cheating each other in the stock market and in similar value-less venues. Twenty-thousand-square-foot homes looking for all the world like participants in a lunatic architectural big-dick contest now clung to the hillsides above the Yellowstone River and out on the grassy floodplains. Bistros and coffee kiosks abounded. "The real West my ass," Joe said aloud as he looked up Miles City way and thought about what was going on there. How soon would the malignancy reach the old bars and stores on Main Street? When would the ranch hands and old-timers be forced out of their watering holes? "Damn fools trash everything they touch. Shit all over a place and on those of us who call it home. God help the bastards if I ever find out I have cancer." He took a small sip of water. "Thank God they can't see what this country really is. With my wonderful luck the useless shits will latch onto rockhounding the way they strangled fly fishing. Dickheads will haul the country away in their four-wheel-drive Cadillacs and Range Rovers one bag of rocks at a time." He spit in the direction of town. "Worthless shits. They produce nothing that matters and ruin what means something to the rest of us." He laughed at his tirade and concentrated on calming down. Turkeys were spooky as hell, had radar for the hate he was broadcasting. Minutes passed and he dropped into the timeless rhythm of the mangled hills.

He turned slowly and peered through a crack in the rocks. "Jesus Christ!" he said to himself. He'd not even heard it coming. The biggest bird he'd ever seen. He looked once more. "Thirty-five pounds. Maybe larger. Beard must be well over a foot if it's an inch. Damn!"

He took five minutes soundlessly moving the .22 into position. He lined the barrel's bead on the turkey's head, on its unblinking eye. He curled his finger around the trigger and began to gently squeeze. Then he stopped and stared as the bird dipped its big head up and down, pecking at something in the spongy moss. He felt like he was being watched. The hairs on the back of his neck stood up. He carefully looked behind him. Nothing. No one. Joe started to pull on the trigger once more, but again he stopped. The feeling of being watched grew stronger and he turned once again. Still nothing. And he watched the bird over the top of the bead on the .22, the turkey unaware of his presence.

"Can't kill this one. Maybe the only bird this size in Montana, hell the whole damn West." He stood up. If turkeys could look stunned, this one did. Standing erect, almost five feet tall, it looked right at Joe then let loose with a series of screaming gobbles as it fled, feathers tucked tight to its thick body, downhill and out of sight.

He could have killed that bird, easy, Joe thought; couldn't bring himself to do it. "Never see anything like that again in my life." He walked over to the spring and looked at the tracks the tom had left in the moist, sandy soil and moss. Three-pronged prints almost as big as his hand etched in the soil and pressed down in the moss, which was rapidly regaining its original form. Droppings as thick as medium cigars. "More than thirty-five pounds. God what a bird."

He stood there on top of Chambers Point for a long time. The sensation of someone watching him passed. He thought about this before saying, "Completely nuts. That's all there is to it."

Joe looked out over the land until well after the sun went down and the eternal, countless stars came out.

At the same time Joe was drawing down on the turkey, several miles northwest of Chambers Point, a lone wolf loped along a game trail following the fresh tracks and droppings of several mule deer that had passed this way not long before. The well-traveled path was worn several inches into the soil and paralleled Philly Joe Coulee. This particular solitary creature dwarfed the gray wolves that ran in the beleaguered Magic, Wigwam, and Camas packs in Glacier Park country or those hapless canine souls that had been reintroduced—more accurately, kidnapped—from their territories somewhere else in the Northwest to be dumped into Yellowstone Park. This wolf picked off a scent riding the cooling southeast wind. The animal stopped and sniffed. The clear odor of man coming down from a rocky point outlined sharply against the sky sent a shiver along its deep tan, gray, and white body. It raised its enormous muzzle into the air for a better taste. The wolf was familiar with the scent, had encountered it for years. In the past, at the first whiff, the merest suggestion of contact with humans, the animal had turned tail and vanished into obscure niches of the obscure country. But not this time. Something in the way this man smelled, and the wolf was capable of telling a man from a woman, some slight coloring around the edges of his scent, stopped the animal in its tracks and caused it to stare for a long time in the direction the wind was coming from. There were the odors that signaled predator and death but there was something more, something wild like the wolf itself, perhaps another animal of the wild with no rules to live by except those of freedom and survival. It turned to drift down into the coulee out of harm's way, looking for one last time up at Chambers Point. And then the four-hundred-pound beast swiftly, silently vanished.

Joe and Mickey were fixing some fence down in the bottom of Mad Woman Gulch. The soil was sandy clay. Several of Joe's peripatetic Angus had pushed against the sagging barbed-wire strands and knocked down some rotted wooden posts in the process. Cattle and the weather were always doing a number on Joe's fence lines. Repairing them was a never-ending chore. The cows had wandered the length of the gulch and up onto the bench above, where they were inexorably heading for the burning coal seams. A massive barbecue in the offing. Elmer had spotted the animals while scanning the land through his high-powered telescope, something he did for hours every day when he wasn't highballing it on the backroads with the Boykins, which were still silent according to Elmer. "Not so much as a yip out of 'em, but I'm hanging in there. They'll break soon, I damn well hope to tell ya," he told Joe over the phone along with the information on his wandering cattle. Joe was having coffee with Mickey at the time. The two of them walked a mile or so, spotted the Angus, and ran them back home, scaring the dumb beasts by yelling and waving their arms. The cattle along with a couple of dozen of their less adventuresome compatriots were now standing in the filthy muck and moss bordering the small stock pond that formed from the meager output of a little off-and-on spring. By July the thing would be nothing more than a small bit of thick, alga-choked soup and cracked mud. A home to millions of flies and a powerful stink.

Joe worked the posthole digger, slammed the blades into the hard ground that lay a couple of feet beneath the clay, twisted the tool around and back and forth with his legs, arms, and shoulders, then squeezed the thing closed so he could extract a cupful of soil. Hard work beneath the sun, but there were only seven old holes to redig. Mickey placed the metal stakes by each hole before dropping them in and kicking rock and dirt around them. Then she used a solid steel breaker bar to tamp down the ground, and repeated the process until each stake was standing upright and rock-solid. From time to time Joe would look up from his work, wipe his sweaty forehead on his shirt-sleeve, then yell an assortment of obscenities at the Angus as they stared back at him with dumb, dark eyes, viscous drool hanging from their mouths in long strings. Sometimes his tirades would scare the creatures to the extent that they would erupt in explosive outbursts of watery green-brown shit that splattered on the ground and into the water. At moments like this he'd think, *Enough to make you give up beef,* then return to slamming the tool into the ground, the sharp metal blades clanging off chunks of rock.

In a couple of hours all the stakes were set. The two of them used a come-along to winch the four rusting strands tight before attaching it to the posts with wire clips that they twisted with pliers. Finished, they walked over to a large ponderosa and dropped down in the shade onto a soft, crunching carpet of needles. Joe pulled a pair of warm beers from the tool kit, popped the tops in a cascade of foam, and handed one to Mickey. They each drained off half and looked at the ocher-lime-colored cutbank across the gulch. Night before last a heavy thunderstorm had dumped an inch of rain amid a hail of lightning, thunder, and tornadic blowings. Common weather on the Workman. A lightning bolt had fried one of Elmer's cows and a gust of wind had crumpled a small chicken coop, releasing incensed and terrified hens clucking all over the place. One of the roosters quartered in a nearby pen was now up on the peak of the barn roof squawking away. Elmer told Joe he was thinking about "Bringing the damn bird down with my thirty-oh-six," but he wasn't sure just yet. Power lines were also down along the roads. Quite a blast. Tons of soil lay in piles and chunks at the bottom of the forty-foot-deep draw, washed and broken away from the deluge.

The rain had scrubbed the air clean of wind-driven dust. Sunlight sparkled off mineral deposits in the earth glittering like diamonds. Quartz and mica. Moving his head to look up toward Elmer's land, something flashed white in the dirt. Joe stared hard at the spot and located what looked like an exposed portion of a large skull stuck in the bank about a dozen feet below the surface. A large dark hole, perhaps an eye socket, stared at him. He walked over to the bank, clambered up so that he was eye-to-eye with the skull. Above him snakes sunning themselves rattled in the grass at the edge of the bank. Steadying himself, Joe began digging in the loosely packed soil around the bones.

"Mickey. I think it's an old buffalo skull," he yelled. "Come over and look." Joe pulled the loose soil from the thing, grasped it with both hands by the jaws, and yanked. The ground at his feet and that holding the skull gave way easily and Joe went flying away from the shelf and down to the bottom of Mad Woman, chunks and buckets worth of dirt piling on top of him. The bison skull cracked him on the head as he crash-landed, knocking him senseless. In an instant Mickey was kneeling over him frantically digging and pushing dirt and rock away. Blood streamed from a large cut in his forehead, the gash forced ever wider by the rapidly rising knot growing above his right eye. He groaned and rolled over the skull, ripping his shirt on one of the bison's horns. He slowly rose to a sitting position, eyes glazed, head lolling on slumped shoulders.

"Shit that hurt." Blood was running into his eye, down his cheek, and onto his jeans. Mickey took her shirt off and ripped it in strips, which she then wrapped around his head and tied off in square knots.

"Are you okay, Joe? God, you look awful."

He wiped his eyes and his head began clearing. What he saw was unexpected, even for Workman country. A huge, probably ancient, buffalo skull lay at his feet. Blood was all over his clothes, the cutbank still crumbled in miniature avalanches of soil and pebbles, and a gorgeous woman was leaning over him naked from the waist up, her firm, white breasts holding forth right in front of his face. Reacting instinctively, he reached forward with one gloved hand, grasped the left one, and leaned forward to suck its erect nipple.

"Ouch, you damn freak." She slapped and pushed his head and hand away in one smooth, hard motion. "Jesus! Is that all you men think about. Hell! I thought you might have a concussion or be bleeding to death, but no. The first thing you think about is sucking my tits." She looked at him with angry eyes that eventually gave way to the beginnings of a smile and laughter. "You are a freak, buddy. God only knows what you really have on your mind when it comes to sex." She looked away, up to where the skull came from, and said softly to herself, out of his hearing, "I guess that's what excites me about you. Not having a clue about what you want from me."

She turned back and commanded, "Take off your shirt and the T-shirt, too."

Joe did as he was told and started in on the belt and zipper of his pants, hoping for the best.

"Not those, you moron, and sure as hell not here in the dirt with you all bloody," she said scornfully. "Men. You're hopeless. I need the T-shirt for me. Can't be bouncing around out here in the open. That crazy Elmer could be anywhere."

Joe shrugged, zipped his fly, and put on his bloodied flannel shirt. Mickey donned his sweaty T-shirt. They both stood up and gathered their bearings, shaking the dirt from themselves, but this was really pointless. Blood, sweat-and-dirt-turned-to mud, and dust covered them. They looked like hard-rock miners after a day's mean labor. A severe headache was making an appearance behind the knot on his head. Waves of sharp pain shot out from his eyes. The cut hurt so bad it felt like it was tearing a wide gash across his face. Mickey retrieved the beers and handed them to Joe. He downed both, hot liquid running out the sides of his mouth and down his chin. A coyote barked not far from them, perhaps a few hundred yards down the gulch. "They must be telepathic," he said. "Every time I even think of touching you, one of those damn dogs starts howling away. Crazy animals are so plugged into this place, I can't even open a can of beer without them knowing about it. Middle of nowhere and no privacy at all."

"What woman in her right mind could resist you," Mickey said as she tried to wipe some dirt and gore from his face. "You're as weird as they come. Grab my boobs after a bloody cave-in. Scare the shit out of your cows. Worship your little brown trout. Commune with coyotes. What else, Joe? What other twisted little things do you have running around in that head?" She wasn't smiling. Wasn't looking mad either. More like curious, like *Where do you want to take me?*

He looked back and pushed down thoughts that were trying to turn themselves into words, pushed them back out of view and only said, "Shit, Mickey," before stooping down to the skull and brushing the dirt off it. With an effort he lifted the mass of soiled bone and shook still more dirt from it. Sand, clay, and rock poured from eye sockets, the mouth, and the neck opening. He held it high. Nearly intact. All of the skull structure, most of the worn teeth, and both horns—large ones that were barely damaged after all these years, centuries. He looked down the rows of teeth to the back. Embedded in some dried mud was a piece of chipped, black stone. He set the skull down and dug at the object with his fingers. Finally he extracted the two-inch piece. Black and shiny like obsidian and formed into a point, a spear point. He could see the scalloped chisel marks, and when he looked again at the back of the bison skull he noticed a shattered edge along the bone.

"Probably made by the hunters," he said as he held out the spear point to show her, gesturing at the damaged bone. "Before horses were introduced, they used to herd the buffalo to cliffs, even small ones like that"—he aimed a finger at the tall cutbank—"and run them over the edge, then finish them off with spears and large rocks, anything handy. Beat them to death. Must have been something to see." He looked at the skull a long time. "As deep as this buffalo was buried in the ground . . . hell, it may be a thousand years old or more, times before the Cheyenne or Crow were out here. Maybe Yanktonai Sioux, but who knows for sure when any of them reached this country.

"Mickey, give me a hand with this. We'll lug it back and clean it up. I want to hang it over the fireplace. My old man would have loved it. Just his kinda thing." They took turns carrying it up Joe's side of Mad Woman Gulch, the other lugging the fencing tools. "Starting to really feel like shit, girl. Let's keep pushing."

"You look bad, Joe. I'll need to put some stitches in that cut for you."

On the way back Mickey noticed huge dog tracks running down the slope they were climbing. She pointed them out to Joe.

"Probably from Coaker's mastiffs running deer. Goddamn those dogs. Elmer's seen them, too. Said the rain makes the tracks look larger than they really are, which already is big." The two continued on, sweating, swearing and trudging back to Joe's place.

On top of a sandstone cliff some miles away the huge wolf picked up the man's scent once again. There was no fear at the taste of human in its nostrils. Only recognition. The animal had worked its way south from Chambers Point as it had done sporadically for some time. Now it was down here following the faint traces of the man's smell. No reason for this behavior surfaced in the wolf's head. It was reacting naturally from external stimuli and internal fires, drives. A wild animal roaming the countryside. The wolf lifted its head and screamed an ungodly howl, a sound not heard on the Workman for a very long time.

Not for more than eighty years and never with this intensity. The cry died on the wind before ever reaching Joe and Mickey as they worked their way through the pines.

Warm, mineral-rich water bubbled up through cracks in the rock, making the hot-tub-sized pool in the smooth stone appear effervescent. The water poured over a narrow gap in the rock and flowed down into a narrow crease in the land, cascading down a series of limestone steps until it reached Mad Woman Gulch, where it disappeared into the porous soil. The hot springs formed at the head of the draw at a place where cracks and fissures allowed the water to push through to the surface. This country was dotted with such warm outbursts of liquid. Joe and Mickey lounged naked in the warmth and sucked in the moist air that tasted of sulfur mixed with the sweet perfume of the grasses, sage, and wildflowers. Hundreds of striped chorus frogs croaked all around them. Night owls boomed not far away, and a lone robin babbled from a tall ponderosa below them. From their positions in the pool they could see out over the tops of the pines growing in the ravine, could see for miles and miles across the rolling, green expanse of the plateau with its multicolored, pine-cloaked bluffs and hills. Mickey had suggested that a long hot soak might ease some of Joe's pain, so the pair had packed a couple of bottles of Merlot and some Honduran cigars. They walked through the trees behind his place and the quarter mile through the new, thick grass that was heavy with cool evening dew. Shedding their clothes, they slipped into the 109-degree water and sighed as one. Mickey opened one of the bottles of wine, the cork giving way with a small pop. She bit off the ends of two cigars, lit them, and handed one to Joe. They sat back and drank in the night sky.

The usual countless stars and planets and galaxies were out, but a growing instrument-dash green glow in the north was beginning to overpower the stars. The luminous haze rose above the horizon and boiled like storm clouds. Suddenly narrow streams of intense green shot far into the night sky and sailed over their heads. Next, curtains of the diaphanous light shimmered across the entire northern horizon. Streaks of brighter green raced through these with an intensity that cast soft green-black shadows over the grass and sage. Joe and Mickey's faces fluoresced in the heavenly radiance. The northern lights. Not the blues, whites, and reds of Alaska, but rather the subtly intense shades of green common to the Workman. They could hear the gentle buzzing of the lights as they flashed in wave after wave across their vision. The water around them bubbled and sparkled as though illuminated from within each molecule.

Joe drank some wine and passed the bottle to Mickey, who did the same. They worked on their cigars, the aromatic smoke rising in dense streams straight into the quiet air.

From down the draw a ball of white light flashed briefly then disappeared behind a small cliff before reappearing much closer. Then the pulsing orb raced up toward them, whizzing over their heads and circling the open meadow that surrounded the springs before racing silently back down from where it came. The frogs went quiet with the appearance of the mysterious stranger.

Joe and Mickey looked at each other and laughed. Not aliens or their spacecraft. Nothing like that. The coulee contained a peculiar electrical charge that triggered Saint Elmo's fire when the humidity and temperature were just right. The ball of heatless flame again tore up the ravine, lighting chokecherry trees, pussy willows, and curious rock outcroppings in its lunatic path. Then the sphere zoomed right across the surface of the pool between the two of them, flashing past in a silent, yet perceivable *whoosh,* before circling and scampering away down the draw.

By now the northern lights were so bright, everything looked as though it were bathed in the smoothest of green sunrises. The ball of Saint Elmo's Fire continued its eccentric orbits. The frogs resumed their croaking, and Joe and Mickey wordlessly enjoyed each other's company and that of the wildly alive Workman Plateau.

The next morning Joe was sitting in his attorney's waiting room. The secretary said that Scott "Kid" Camp was running late in his meeting with the two directors of Breezy Sage Development. The nickname *Kid* had something to do with goats during Camp's youth. Joe had never bothered finding out precisely what that might have been. The secretary looked at Joe's swollen, bandaged head and blackening eye but didn't say a word. Her dour look spoke for her. *How tall was the bar stool you fell off of?* she might have said. Joe stared her down from his sunken position in a well-worn leather chair. He scanned the six-month-old copies of *Sports Illustrated, ABA Barrister,* and *Dudes & Savages,* a yuppie rag if he'd ever seen one. Thousand-dollar boots, ridiculous versions of western hats, even more expensive clothes, and exorbitantly priced watches and turquoise jewelry. He didn't know anyone who dressed like that, had never seen anyone wear any of those ostentatious items around town, that is until the door to Kid's office opened and out walked a pair of well-tanned men in their midthirties. They were wearing those same boots, immaculate oversized hats adorned with enough pheasant feathers to stuff a pillow, brand-new pressed jeans, custom-made western shirts, gold watches, turquoise bracelets, and long-cut suede coats.

"We'll take care of the covenants and that little detail on the earnest money, Kid," one of them said with a voice that reflected the arrogance of those who have more money than they know what to do with and are proud of it, the rest of humankind being merely odious creatures that must be tolerated, barely, and preferably at a distance. The pair made money selling nothing but transient enthusiasm and when they'd milked a concept dry, fabricated another one. *Money for nothing,* Joe thought. They glanced at Joe in his faded jeans, worn denim shirt, and scuffed boots. Then just like that, he wasn't there for them anymore. He was not of their kind, so they banished him from their vision, from their minds. He was trash and proud of it. "See you next week, Kid, when we get back from California."

Kid said, "So long," vigorously shook their hands, and turned to Joe.

"Boy, what bar stool did you tumble off of?"

Joe smiled, painfully. His head hurt despite the two Percodans Mickey had given him with his morning coffee. They walked into the recently vacated office, the room reeking of expensive cologne, and sat down. Kid eased into a cushy chair behind a massive walnut desk cluttered with abstracts, a box of Titleist golf balls, an antique postage scale, and yellow legal pads. Joe dropped into a comfortable wingback job on the other side of the huge piece of furniture.

"How in the hell can you represent those clowns?" asked Joe. "That piece-of-shit gated community with its ricky-tick, cutesy condos and golf course is going to destroy twenty miles of the Workman. Damn good trout water, not to mention the birds and deer. Now only some rich out-of-state assholes will get to fish it. That is if there are any trout left in it after they get done spraying all those chemicals on the greens. And then we've got to contend with their bullshit around town and a bunch of other crap to boot. Maybe some aging pretty-boy director can make a compelling western movie about a man who dances with golf carts." Joe looked past Kid out the window at people walking along the street. "There's no escaping them. Makes me sick."

"Community needs the money and so do I," said Kid. "They pay well and the development will provide jobs around here, and that's that."

"Yeah, and the West sure needs one more golf course. Dumb-ass sport. My idea of a dream vacation. Head out to the best country anywhere and chase a little white ball around. Jesus." Joe laughed. Kid wasn't laughing.

The two men stared at each other in silence and Joe thought, *Last time I talk with this sellout piece of shit and pay for the privilege in the process.*

"Joe, I'll make this short and simple for both our sakes," said Kid as he lit up a Marlboro, exhaling a series of nearly perfect smoke rings that drifted across the desk. "The wording in your papers is unique to say the least, but the bottom line is your father sold off the mineral rights to Northern High Plains, and Dark Star bought them out years ago. Though you still own the water rights. From the language I'd have to say that he didn't want you to know about it. Didn't want anyone to know the details until he was dead and buried. Whenever the Consortium decides to dig up the coal on your land—or natural gas or oil, for that matter—they can. No ifs, ands, or buts. They own more of your place than you do. When, if ever, they decide to proceed, they can do pretty much what they want provided they adhere to what passes for environmental regs in Montana. When they're done, they're done, and they aren't required to do much in the way of reclamation, of putting back the land the way they found it.

Smooth some hills a bit and fill in the holes some. Haul out their machinery and junk. That's about it."

Joe sat in the chair stunned. He couldn't think of anything to say. His mind reeled at the finality of Kid's words. The realization that his father had lied to him and sold him out, not even that registered. That would sink in later after some bourbon. The only thing that ran through his mind was the fact that someday the land he loved, his land, would be torn up, ripped apart, and the coal hauled away to be burned for power.

"Nothing you can do?" he asked.

"Nothing anyone can do," said Kid as he stubbed out his cigarette in a marble ashtray. "Sorry to be the bearer of these ill tidings, but I'm not going to waste your money beating a dead horse. All you can do is accept it and move on. It's a tough deal, but the agreements are binding and they're bulletproof. I had a partner look it over and he came to the same conclusion. Your father apparently did the deal with a guy named Bill Foxen. He's a corporate VP for Dark Star. Bill Foxen. I've heard some about him. Tough as nails when it comes to business. Doesn't believe in compromise and knows his stuff. I'll include his contact number in Denver when I send you a breakdown of the deeds and agreements with Northern High Plains that might help clear things up some for you, along with the bill for my time. Check around with other attorneys if you like. Just a waste of money, in my opinion."

Joe looked at Kid, stood up without saying anything or shaking hands, wandered through the waiting room and out the front door. His feet carried him to that tall bar stool that was waiting for him in The Mint across the street. He ordered a double of Jim Beam and stared at his reflection in the smoky mirror behind the bar. The one Foxen had looked into long ago, as had Joe's father many times over the years. A few drinks and a hundred cigarettes later, Joe was still looking vacantly into the mirror when he saw his face transform into that of his father laughing at him, then Mickey's doing the same thing, then once again his father, this time sneering, then the reflection was his own grim, injured self.

"Enough of this shit," Joe muttered. He pushed away from the bar, leaving a stack of bills next to his glass, and drove back home. The sun was still high in the sky. Midafternoon in early May. A long bank of dark clouds was boiling up over the Sanders. The wind was blowing cold out of the west.

They began working on the coal-hauling rail line on the last day of spring, much sooner than anyone, including Dark Star, had expected. Years of political legwork, surveying, spreading a bit of cash in all the right places, a leap in the price of natural gas, especially Canadian gas—all these combined to push the process for granting right-of-way along the Workman River far ahead of projections. Environmental assessment approvals, even the purchasing of the last few remaining parcels of private land, all happened virtually simultaneously. Everything was neatly wrapped up in a couple of frantic weeks in May. Pete Kilduff and the company's legal minions worked long hours to sew up the deal. Graves owned approximately three hundred yards of land along the planned path of the tracks down by the river. He adamantly refused to sell, no matter what the price. He'd slammed down the phone on Kilduff and refused to meet with the man anywhere or anytime. But when it was discovered that his holdings stopped well short of the water with room to spare on government river corridor holdings, the Consortium made a few minor adjustments and shifted the planned route ever so slightly closer to the river and over Joe's little trout stream. The tracks would run across the last few yards of the tiny creek before it joined with the river, but not cross any of his land. Joe's creek would soon be flowing through a galvanized steel culvert and pouring into the Workman, like water running from a large faucet.

To say that Joe was angry was an understatement. He saw the proposed line between McCoy and Miles City for what it truly was. One of the last nails in the coffin of a wild Workman Plateau. Carefully planned and landscaped communities for the well moneyed, that same group purchasing ranches to be run at a loss for tax advantages, plans to pave the country's backroads, and on and on. Good country now being brutalized and tamed by men, machinery, and greed. Mule deer, ponderosa forest, a free-flowing river, coyotes, sage grouse, rattlesnakes, turkeys, Graves, Yoter, all of them being exterminated in a relentless miasmic avalanche of technological lust.

"First the fucking train tracks, then what?" he'd say to Mickey or Elmer or anyone else who would listen. "Why the hell not level the bluffs and banks on the west side of the river and build another goddamn golf course? Irrigate the abortion with water from the river. The hell with the catfish, browns, sauger, smallmouths, and the game. Hell, they could hire Northern Cheyennes from the reservation for caddies. Nice half-ass western touch for the Californians that would be. 'Hey Lone Wolf, wanna hand me my five-iron there, Chief.' Got to have another golf course, that's for damn sure." And so forth. And his anger would grow and boil and he'd walk the two-plus miles from his home to a cliff overlooking the river and the land where the tracks would be and he'd stare and swear and then, completely lost in his rage, he'd scream, a mad, wild sound like the lone wolf he now heard every night sometime after midnight. And he'd start kicking stones and dirt over the precipice and then heave larger stones and then push and strain against boulders lying near the edge, his face purple with the effort, veins bulging along the sides of his head, and then he'd cackle madly as the weight of the rock crashed and tore through the survey stakes several hundred feet below him. Then one day he stopped in the middle of his efforts and glanced around at the remaining rocks, some the size of fifty-five-gallon oil drums, and he looked from the path of the proposed rail line far below him and then back at the boulders, and then he laughed silently to himself and said, "Why the hell not? What happens, happens." Then he walked back home and drank a lot of whiskey.

★ ★ ★

Meanwhile Dark Star went about the business of punching the rail line through. They hoped to complete the work before the winter weather, ugly storms screaming down from the Arctic, closed in sometime in November. Piles of cement railroad ties, miles of heavy steel track, powerful graders, earth-hauling rigs the size of houses, lots of explosives, track-laying machinery, D-9s, all of this stuff began accumulating in the company's yard at McCoy. The equipment was painted black with yellow-and-red insignias. A sinister army preparing to launch its invasion all along the Workman Front. War. War against the land, the river, the people who lived here, war against a way of life. And Dark Star was planning to win and quickly, too.

That last day of spring was miserably wet with dense, filthy gray clouds choking out the sun and drowning the land in a thick, cold drizzle. You couldn't see more than a quarter mile in any direction. But Dark Star began blasting away at the bluffs and the hills and rock outcrops that blocked the path of the new rail line. And the huge earth haulers belched and roared their way up to the tons of dynamited rubble and sage and splintered ponderosa and juniper and willow and then hauled the chunks and pieces of the shattered Workman Plateau away to be dumped in the canyonlike pits left from the strip mining over by McCoy. The river ran muddy brown from the work. Greasy slicks of oil, diesel, and hydraulic fluid floated on the water's surface, reflecting the day's dim light in malignant rainbows.

Graves observed the devastation from a rocky point far above the men and their machinery. He watched in silence. Motionless.

One week later, a warm, sunny day, Workman County sheriff Egyptian Healy pulled up in front of Joe's place in his cruiser. He was followed by Pete Kilduff in a Dark Star pickup. The Consortium needed the water on Graves's land to pump onto the burning seams of coal over at Yoter's. Drilling in on an angle from Elmer's land was proving difficult. The underground water was not where the original soundings had placed it. A pair of time-consuming, expensive dry holes had made this clear. The Consortium wanted the water right now and they wanted to begin surveying work on Joe's land, not so much for the coal, but rather as a legal excuse to begin constructing the haul road from Elmer's land through Mad Woman Gulch up the rise past Joe's house and on down the relatively smooth gully where the little trout stream ran. Dark Star could do this. They had all the papers and peripheral legal documentation, but they needed to serve Joe with the action papers to avoid the week-or-so delay that obtaining a court order would entail. The company was patient, had long-range plans for mining all over this part of Montana and much of Wyoming, but once it decided to move, then that action happened fast. Get on and well into the land before any media-generated news stirred up the hordes of environmental groups waiting out there for a cause, a sexy issue, to hang their nattering, self-righteous hats on. The conservationists, preservationists, environmentalists, whatever they called themselves, Kilduff preferred "posy fuckers," could always be outspent or outmaneuvered or, as a last resort, outwaited. Everyone in the industry was aware of the fact that most of these crusaders had the attention span of a herd of gerbils. But Dark Star wanted to get up to speed on this next phase of its southeastern Montana strip-mining operation right now, so they prevailed upon the sheriff to do his duty.

Egyptian Healy—he had family from Cairo, Illinois, hence the nickname—was an old friend of Joe's. They'd gone to school together in the one-room building that sat beside a red dirt road halfway between the Wyoming state line and the county seat of Garland, population 502 and sinking. Joe and Egyptian had hunted together, screwed the same girls in high school, and had more than a few drinks together in the years since. Kilduff knew all this and figured Healy had at least an outside chance of getting close enough to Joe to serve the papers. The sheriff had his doubts and wondered if Joe was as outraged as he'd seen him in The Mint recently and heard about from people in Drew and from ranchers out on the plateau. He knew all about Joe's temper. Like the time he'd shot an overaggressive Kirby Vacuum Cleaner salesman in the foot when the guy had refused to leave at once. The salesman had been forcing himself on every rancher in the county and when Healy turned up an outstanding warrant from Toledo, Ohio, concerning the man taking earnest money from people back there for promised aluminum siding jobs that somehow never got much beyond the stage of tacking a square or two of the stuff on the sides of the hapless victims' homes, well, Healy did what needed to be done to protect Joe, an accidental discharge of the .30-30 or something. He also managed to have the Kirby man extradited back to Ohio. Case closed. But that was only one example of Joe's temper and there'd been a number of others, though he'd been behaving himself ever since he'd started sleeping with that Krietner woman. So Healy was more than a bit edgy when he pulled up in front of Joe's place and turned off the engine. He left his hat on the seat, checked to make sure his revolver was unstrapped, took off his sunglasses, and stepped out of the car. Joe was standing on the back porch steps smiling and holding the .30-30.

"'Morning Egyptian. See you dragged some Dark Star scum in your wake." Joe levered a round into the gun's chamber. "I'm not talking to him. Said all I want to say to anyone on the matter." He stepped down to the bottom step.

"Joe, knock it off. I've got to serve you this paper or the court's gonna do the same thing up in Garland. You know how that old fart Thacker is," Healy said with as much calmness and good-neighbor spirit as he could muster, which wasn't much. He was terrified. His shirt was sweat-soaked under his arms and down the back. Joe's eyes were narrowed and his entire bearing was that of a man ready for violence. "Damnit Joe. We've been friends for over forty years and

Judge Thacker's only gonna side with Dark Star." The sheriff jerked a thumb in the black truck's direction. "And he'll probably find a way to fine you some in the process. Hell, he's never gotten over you popping that salesman." Healy forced a weak laugh.

Graves laughed, too. A mean sound.

"Shit, Egyptian." After a pause he started laughing. "*Shit Egyptian*. That sounds damn funny to me." He laughed again, a wild sound that rose in pitch, and he began rocking back and forth as he did so. Healy took a step forward.

"Hold it right there." Now Graves stepped down to the ground. "Those Dark Star bastards aren't messing with my land. I don't care if my old man did sell away the rights. And I don't give a rat's ass about the law either, even when it comes dressed up looking like you."

The two men faced off in silence for what seemed like an eternity to Healy, who thought for sure this was his day to die. Joe looked up from Healy to a large raven sitting on top of a tall ponderosa behind the shed. The bird was motionless but occasionally let out with a grating *cruck, cruck, cruck,* a sound that faded quickly in the stillness. He stared at that bird a long time. Perhaps ten minutes. Then the sheriff thought he detected a shift in Joe's mood. *For the better?* Healy asked himself. *God, get me out this one and I promise I'll only have six drinks at the bar today. I promise, God.*

Graves took another step and laughed that weird, frightening laugh again.

"Give me your damn paper, Egyptian." Joe held out his hand. "Come on. I won't shoot you. Maybe that lame prick in the truck, but not you."

Healy edged forward and thrust the paper to Joe at arm's length while his body involuntarily leaned in the other direction, closer to the perceived shelter of the cruiser. Joe took the document. Shook it open with his free hand, the rifle now clasped in the other and hanging just below his left hip. He read the paper carefully and looked up.

"You're served, Joe . . . and . . . and . . . godda . . . goddamnit I'm sorry about this," stammered Healy. "It's all changing 'round here and I . . . I hate this goddamn job. Had my fill. No way am I running again."

"Relax, Egyptian. I know," Joe said calmly. "Go tell that jerk in the truck to come up here. I won't shoot him. If I was up to that, he'd be dead by now. Rumor is the pricks want to pay me for my water to put out that little inferno over on Elmer's. Brain-dead idiots. That coal's been burning forever and my water isn't going to change that any, but if the morons want to pay for the privilege of indulging their absolute stupidity, who am I to stand in their way? My place is history anyway, thanks to the old man." *And so much for my trout stream,* he thought. *I'll miss that, but I might as well make some money out of this mess if I can. My land and the Workman are about to be destroyed anyway and I can't stop it. Damn all of this.*

Healy looked at Joe and wondered at the change. He'd never in a million years would have imagined that Joe would roll over like this. He was up to something. Healy was certain of it, but he just wanted to get the hell out of there alive. The sheriff walked back to the truck, each step an effort in concentration. His shirt was completely soaked with sweat that smelled of fear and old whiskey.

Kilduff had been taking all this in through the open window of the truck's cab. He looked up at Healy.

"He playing it straight, Sheriff, or's this a setup?"

"He'd of killed you by now if he was going to, sir. Go on up and say what you've got to say and I'll be there with you. Take it easy and let's just get things settled and get out of here. Okay?"

"That's why we're here, Sheriff." Kilduff got out of the black truck and walked up to within ten feet of Joe, who was still holding the rifle in one hand and the order in another. Healy stood to one side and slightly behind Kilduff, right hand on his gun.

"No need for that, Egyptian. I hate this asshole and his damn company, but I'm not going up to Deer Lodge for shooting this slime or you either. Hell, a damn head shot wouldn't kill you anyway." All three men laughed. "Have a seat," he added, waving in the direction of an old weathered table and some chairs gathered on one side of the porch. The ancient bison skull, now cleaned up, was placed in the middle of the round table. "I'll go in and grab some beers and whiskey and don't give me any shit about not drinking while on duty, Egyptian. We both know you got enough booze in that car to light up half the Workman." They all laughed again. The mood seemed almost convivial, but Healy knew better. Joe had never backed down on anything, ever.

Joe returned with a six-pack of Pabst and a two-thirds-full bottle of Jim Beam.

"Make do without glasses?" asked Joe, looking at Kilduff. "Egyptian's like me. A glass just slows down the process." He cracked a grin in the direction of the sheriff, whose complexion had settled down from purple to merely apoplectic.

"Fine with me, Joe," said Kilduff as he took a drink of whiskey from the offered bottle, then popped the tab on the beer and drained a good bit of it. "That skull looks old. Where'd you find it?"

Joe glanced at the relic and said, "Around here, but let's can the small talk. Get to the point." He looked across to Kilduff, who nodded in agreement. A strong acrid, sooty blast from the burning coal over at Elmer's land drifted over the three men. Then a slight breeze worked through the ponderosas and cleared the air.

"Your father didn't do right by you in my opinion, and the company always prefers to do business up front and make everyone happy—"

"Cut the shit, Kilduff. We both know that all you care about is the coal and the money. Leave my old man out of it and make your offer." Joe took a swig of bourbon, passed the bottle to Healy, and lit a smoke, one of Mickey's Newports.

Healy gulped down the whiskey like a man long stranded in the middle of a burning desert who is finally offered a jug of cold water. Then he handed the bottle to Kilduff, who took another drink.

"Business it is," the Dark Star man said. "We need your water to cool things out over on Yoter's place. Should work according to our engineers, and we want to get at that coal now."

"Couldn't steal it from me with that sidewinder drilling act of yours, could you?" said Joe calmly.

"Business is business, Joe, and you wouldn't talk with us. We had to act," said Kilduff. He looked at the pack of cigarettes, then at Joe, who nodded. Kilduff pulled one out, lit up, and inhaled deeply. He exhaled while continuing, the smoke easing out around his words. "We'll give you fifty thousand up front and five hundred for every million gallons we pump."

Graves looked long and hard at Kilduff, had a sip of whiskey, put out his cigarette and lit another.

"Make it seventy-five and a thousand," he said.

"Done. I'll have the agreement and a certified check for the seventy-five thousand and ten thousand advance on the water we'll use ready in the office tomorrow morning. You can pick it up then."

"Bring all of that here and then we're done," Joe said.

"All right and while we're at it, as you can see from the order, we're going to begin surveying for coal under your land and laying out the haul road, too. If you like we'll route it as far from your place as we can, but work begins tomorrow. You understand?" It was Kilduff's turn to stare long and hard.

"Yeah, Kilduff. I do. My place is long gone and so am I," said Graves. He took a slash of the booze, handed the remains to Healy, got up and returned with another partially full bottle. "I'm sick of you and your company's bullshit. My coal's down deep. You're not after it right now. You want the haul road for Elmer's coal. Hell, you'll never put those fires out in a million years, but take your best shot." He laughed quietly. "Guys like you have killed the Workman. Damn good country and you bastards don't know it."

"I understand," said Kilduff. He got to his feet and indicated that Healy should do the same.

"No. No you don't," said Graves as he stood and backed away from the table. "Your kind never does and never will." He looked at Kilduff, who knew enough not to offer his hand. "Bring the papers yourself. There won't be any trouble. My word on that."

"Around nine then," said Kilduff. He got in the truck, backed up, and drove away.

Healy was already halfway in the cruiser and added, "Thanks, Joe. All I can say is thanks." He drove off.

Joe looked back up at the raven on top of the ponderosa. *Cruck, cruck, cruck.* He picked up the rifle, drew a bead on the black bird, and levered round after round until the gun was empty. Pieces of the mangled raven fell through the long needles and plopped on the ground as the noise from the shooting died among the trees. The smell of gunpowder was thick. Some feathers rocked back and forth on the air as they drifted slowly downward.

"Shouldn't of done that," he said to no one. He grabbed the whiskey and went inside.

Graves stopped his aged pickup in the dusty turnaround at Elmer's. Part of the exhaust pipe had broken off on the way over, so the old man had heard him coming from a long way off and was outside to greet him. Sixteen curly spaniels' burnt umber eyes bright with life trooped out the big screened door and with obvious dignity down the steps, floppy ears hanging limply at the sides of their heads. Then all of them seated themselves in a semicircle behind their master. No barking, no wagging tails.

"See your dogs are still at it, Elmer," said Joe, who couldn't completely stifle his laughter.

"Laugh your fool ass off for all I care." Elmer turned and flicked the well-chewed stub of his cigar over the dogs, ashes and embers raining down on the Boykins. They never moved. "I'm damn near tempted to starve this silent disobedience out of 'em, but I can't bring myself to it. Not yet anyway." He turned on his dogs. "Not yet, but that day is damn sure coming. Hear me?" They didn't even twitch a muscle. Joe broke up.

"I know. I know. When you look at it, it's a damn funny situation I've got going here, but Jesus, this lame-brained behavior . . . I just don't know."

"Elmer, those dogs were bred to run. All that energy. You'd think they'd explode after all this time," said Joe as he lit a smoke.

"Well, I'll let you in on a little secret." Elmer looked behind him at the dogs sitting at attention, all their yellow eyes fixed on the distance of the plateau as the land glided through the orange and purple shades of sunset. He walked up to Joe, leaned forward, and spoke in a soft voice. "They don't know this, but I'm on to them. Last few nights I've been sitting up in the dark looking out by my bedroom window and you know what I saw?"

"No, Elmer. What?"

"Not so loud, damnit." Elmer leaned closer. "Soon as those damn mongrels think I'm asleep, soon as they hear me snoring, they head off the damn porch and run all over the place. I'm not sleeping mind you. I fake the snoring."

"Elmer, does any of this strike you as at least a little bit crazy? I mean, you're up in your room in the dark pretending to be asleep to fool your dogs. You might want to look at this situation some."

"Up yours, Joe. This is war and it's been going on ever since man first began domesticatin' dogs. War. They want to rule the world. Look at them. They think they're some kind of dignitaries and I should be so honored just to be in their high and lordly damn presence," said Elmer, much louder now, but he caught himself, pulled a big green cigar from a shirt pocket, bit off one end, and torched the thing with his lighter. He turned and exhaled a dense cloud of foul-smelling smoke in the spaniels' direction, yelling, "War, you mangy pieces of shit, and I'm going to win. Understand this one right now every goddamn one of you. Me. Elmer Yoter ain't going to be broken by a bunch of nitwit, pea-brained pieces of shit like you." He scuffed dirt and gravel in the dogs' direction. Nothing. "Bird season's coming up and you'd better lose this shit well before then or I'll go out and buy myself a pair of springers. Now there's a real dog fit for a man."

One of the Boykins blinked an eye. Elmer turned to Joe and said, "See? See that. The oldest one blinked. I'm winning, damnit. I knew it. I just fuckin' knew it."

"Elmer, one dog blinked in what, two months. Maybe he had something in his eye?" laughed Joe, who was actually a bit concerned for Elmer's mental well-being.

"No way, Joe. It's a damn sure sign. A break in the wall," roared Elmer as he puffed away on his stogie. He turned back and whispered, "I see 'em through the window and they run and play all night. 'Round and 'round the barn, across those fields all the way to the burnin' coal and back again. All night when they think I'm out cold."

"Whatever you say Elmer. They're your dogs," said Graves.

"Come morning they're sitting on the porch all in a goddamn row, pretty as you please, waiting for this old fart to fill their bowls with food." He walked back over to the dogs, pausing in front of every one of them long enough to cast a withering stare into the eyes of each Boykin. He stopped, bent over, and glared at the oldest one, whom Elmer called Oakley for some unknown reason. The others were nameless. *Sure as shit, it did blink,* thought Joe. "Damn shit that goes on around here, nobody would believe me," he said. "I'm beginning to think you and those dogs read each other's minds or something."

Elmer straightened up and flashed a wide grin. "Won't be long now, Joe. See what I mean. They're cracking. When Oakley goes, they all will go, and real damn soon, too. Tumble like dominoes, one after the other. Canine mind, even sixteen addled pieces of shit like these all hooked up together, are no match for me." He tapped his temple with his forefinger and strode into the house.

"I can see that, Elmer," Joe yelled after him. "The intellectual level of energy around here must be similar to what it feels like at Yale. Hell, Oxford."

"Screw you, Joe." He came out with a bottle of whiskey, the currency of social exchange on the Workman. "Damn fine night. Thought we'd share a little of this out here." Elmer passed the booze to Joe. "Heard that you found out 'bout your father selling the rights. Damn hard piece of news to take, all the way down the line." He looked at Joe in a way that let him know how bad he thought it was, that he cared and was with Joe in this, whatever *this* turned out to be. The smell of burning coal mingled with sage filled the evening.

"Thanks Elmer." Joe hit the bourbon. "Damn well tore me up and pissed me off. Didn't think Dad would ever do that to me. Always thought he was honest with me about things that mattered. But what the hell. I was wrong again. Nothing new. And then that Dark Star asshole Kilduff telling me he was going after my coal the other day"—Joe paused and looked up at the sky to all the stars coming out. "Got some money for my water, though. Maybe I'll go down to Mexico, to those mountains Dad and Wimp went to . . ." He scuffed a boot in the dirt before asking, "You knew about this all along, didn't you, Elmer?"

"Yeah, Joe, I did," said Elmer as he took the offered bottle from his friend. "Your father never told me, but I knew. Live out here in all this space, all this openness"—he swung his hand around to take in miles and miles of the Workman Plateau—"and you get so damn open yourself that there ain't no such thing as a secret. Drove me crazy when I first realized it, but I learned to live with it." A pack of coyotes howled. "Them damn things not only read minds, they see into the future and they know for good and goddamn sure all hell's going to break loose around here. I know it, too." Elmer stared off in the direction of the howling, which had devolved into a series of barks and coyote laughs.

You got it all right about everything in this country, thought Joe as he lit another cigarette.

"Damn straight I do, Joe," said Elmer while looking right through Graves. Then he broke off the gaze with a cracked, yellow-toothed smile and passed the whiskey back. "Look, those Dark Star assholes can go pump the entire flaming Fort Peck Reservoir onto my coal. It'll still be burning good and goddamn bright from now until doomsday. Only thing that'll stop it is one hell-mad, ball-buster of a storm."

Joe thought, *It's coming. It's coming one way or another. I can feel it, too.*

"Damn straight it's coming," bellowed Elmer at the sky. "And I wouldn't miss the son of a bitch for all the bonded whiskey in Kentucky, buddy. The idiot assholes always say nobody gets outta here alive. Well, that ain't it, damnit. What the goddamn fools are picking at, without knowing it, is that no one gets outta here easy. Learn that little tune and life ain't so pissing tough." He spat out some chewed cigar.

The two men silently shared their friendship and apprehensions in the gathering dark. The coyotes howled and then all was silent. Joe and Elmer drank and smoked without talking.

Then once again that lone, wild, ancient howl rocked across the plateau, a long, deep, terrible moan from the animal Joe heard every night. And all of the Boykins answered as one, a sonorous response to a wildness the dogs shared with the large, lone wolf standing out there somewhere invisible in the dark distance.

Elmer looked at the dogs, then off in the direction of the wolf's call.

"That's what all this goofy shit is about. The dogs. The snakes. The burning coal. You and Mickey screwing by Wimp's grave. All of it. That wolf's the sign."

The dogs were quiet again and motionless. Elmer stood watching the moon rise.

It's coming our way, buddy and soon. You and I are in it alone. Nobody else but us and that's it. Together in this mess, is what Joe imagined he heard inside his head. He said, "I understand now, Elmer."

"You always did, Joe, just takes hard times to bring it out of some of us."

The two men let their gazes wander out over the plateau, now glowing silver beneath the moon.

He was rolling down the road between his place and Elmer's as the sun broke above the plateau. Intense yellow-white light shimmered beside the long dark shadows cast by ancient, eroded volcanic cones rising up from the plateau, the scene further complicated when the brightness was fractured into gleaming slivers and diffuse shadows as it cut through the long needles of the ponderosas growing next to the road. This panoply of light and dark blurred and burned his whiskey-bloodshot eyes, making the high-speed cruise something of an adventure. A thick cloud of dust rose behind the old truck as it roared along the red dirt road at well over sixty miles an hour. Joe had the windows cranked down. The cool morning air rushing through the cab soothed his hungover head. Totally lost in the effort it took to keep the pickup from careening into a tree, he failed to notice the flashing red, white, and blue lights behind him. The oscillating whining wail of the siren caught his attention, though.

"Shit," he said while pulling over on a wide spot of the road. The cop car slid to a stop several car lengths behind in a curtain of dust that swept over the truck. He heard its door open and slam shut, then the sound of boots crunching in the dirt. "What now?" he said to himself. "Speeding out here? No way."

In his cracked rearview mirror he watched as several skewed images of the patrolman approached, a tall, lean fellow wearing the obligatory aviator sunglasses and a flat, wide-brimmed cop hat. Something looked wrong with the picture to Joe, and it took several seconds for the incongruity of the image to register in his Jim Beam–addled mind. This was not a Montana cop. The car had Wyoming markings and the man wore that state's uniform.

"What the hell's going on here?" he said, again to himself, as he fished for his driver's license and vehicle registration buried somewhere in his wallet. "Did I turn the wrong way coming out of Elmer's?" He glanced at the sun rising higher to his right, the east. "Nope. I'm aiming north."

The Wyoming cop said, "'Morning monsieur. May I see you license please?" He pronounced it *lee-saunce*. He was standing a few feet from Joe, dark glasses now slipped down to the tip of his nose. A touch of Texas in the guy's voice. West Texas, maybe.

"Here, officer." Joe proffered the requisite papers. "What gives? I was only doing sixty."

"Monsieur, the speed limit in Wyoming on unimproved roads is forty-five miles per hour or approximately seventy kilometers per hour. You were clearly exceeding both these measures of velocity."

Shit, this fool doesn't even know he's in Montana. And what's with this monsieur and kilometer crap? The cop was a dead ringer for actor Harry Dean Stanton, dark hair and eyes, bony face, sunken cheeks. Joe wondered if he should tell the man that he was in the wrong state, and he did, politely pointing out that he'd spent the night at a friend's place four miles back down the road behind him, that this place was two-point-four miles north of the Wyoming line, and that they were presently standing six miles into Montana.

"Please look, officer, up there at the green mileage indicator over there," suggested Joe, pointing to a small green sign about a hundred yards ahead of them.

The cop glanced up from Joe's license, or *lee-saunce,* and looked at the sign. Looked at Joe and then back to the mileage marker just as a raven dropped down from the sky and landed on top of it. The bird croaked once and then stared at the two men.

"I appear to have overstepped my boundaries, here, monsieur. Montana mileage marker number six. An honest and sincere mistake on my part I assure you. May I give you back your *lee-saunce* and vehicle registration with my heartfelt apologies?" The cop handed them back to Joe and bowed slightly with an ingratiating smile on his face. Joe took them from the man, thought of making a smartass crack, and then thought better of it.

"You're not from around here, are you, officer?'

"No monsieur. I'm from Paris, Texas."

Joe couldn't hold back on this one and said, "Yeah, I saw the movie."

"Beg your pardon, Monsieur Graves? I don't seem to understand."

"Nothing. Nothing at all," said Joe. "How'd you end up here?"

"My brother-in-law is a lieutenant with the Wyoming State Police down in Cheyenne at headquarters and he helped me find employment up here. It's a big break for me."

"I can see that." In Joe's hungover, broken-down condition all of this almost made sense, seemed a part of the normal day-to-day on the Workman. Almost. The confused cop was staring at him with a slightly crazed look that really did remind him of Harry Dean Stanton in that movie, the part at the beginning where he's hoofing it away from everything out along some lonesome rail line. *Jesus,* he thought, *this life keeps getting weirder and weirder. It just doesn't let up.* Joe wasn't even going to touch the French accent mingled with the Texas drawl. *God only knows where this Paris, Texas, bullshit will wind up.*

"Monsieur, may I ask you a question, *s'il vous plait?'*

Joe almost said *Shoot,* but caught himself. "Ask away."

"When I was in Texas I would watch the Weather Channel on television and it would always show these most horrible storms in Wyoming and Montana. Wind, rain, snow. Most terrible. I've been having the pleasure of working in this beautiful country for three months now and still no storms. Is there a meteorological anomaly occurring in this land? Something I am unaware of?"

I have no idea what the hell you're aware of buddy, thought Joe. "No officer," said Joe, shaking his head. "Sometimes things blow calm for days on end in this country, then all hell breaks loose, and take my word on it, all hell is going to break loose around here pretty damn soon."

The Wyoming cop thought on this one for a little while then looked back to Joe.

"I think I see now," he said calmly as he pushed his glasses back up the bridge of his nose. "Thank you very much for your time and patience. Again, my most sincere apologies for having interrupted your travels. Good day, monsieur."

"Good day, yourself, officer."

The cop got in his cruiser, turned it around, and headed back south in the direction of Wyoming.

"What in the hell is going on around here?" Joe started up the truck and drove on home. The raven watched him as he disappeared around the bend, then croaked once more and abruptly lifted into the air and vanished.

He was dead tired when he got home. His joints and muscles ached. Lately he'd been feeling perpetually exhausted and he couldn't hold a thought in his head for more then a few seconds. Dizziness was part of his life. The stress from the past few months coupled with the late night with Elmer and his crazy dogs had done him in. He had felt better after talking and drinking with the old man. He always did; it was a form of minor salvation to learn he had a friend who saw things the way he did, the way he'd been trying to deny for years. Yeah, he was nuts and yeah, so was Elmer, but so what? He'd take Elmer's mad loyal friendship over the self-centered superficial phoniness that passed for the real thing these days. He'd take that anytime. The way he saw life these days he figured pretty much the whole world was insane. Tear up the land, rip out the coal, displace people who lived here for generations, and for what? Burn the stuff to generate power to run the tools of ignorance that drove the electronic age that was controlling all of us. That made sense the same way dumping raw sewage in the oceans and rivers did, or the Japanese, and us, clear-cutting Western Canada and now Siberia. Who needs forests? The whole premise of existence, the lies, the greed, the waste, the posturing social games, all of the ego-centered crap was completely crazy. To pretend otherwise, that was what was insane; to go on pretending that acquiring BMWs, thousands of acres of land, Persian rugs, young classy women, all the shit that meant nothing to him, that was what was truly off the wall. Without value. Not real. Chasing that, the thought of being obsessed with all the acquisition, that to him was madness, death of the spirit. He wanted none of it. Sharing a nice fire in the middle of nowhere in the still of the night, passing around a bottle and talking some with a good friend like Elmer, money couldn't buy it. "And thank God for that," he said aloud to the empty kitchen. He poured a little bourbon in a glass, diluted it with some water, and drained off the drink while looking out the window. Some black tufts of feathers from the raven he'd murdered the other day were trapped in one of the eye sockets of the bison skull. They quivered at the slightest movement of air. *Why did I do that. Not like me at all. Kill something for the mean pleasure of it. Not right at all.* He shook his head and placed the glass in the sink. He pulled off his boots and left them by the table as he did his shirt and socks. The jeans dropped behind the living room couch as he paused briefly before entering his bedroom. The shades were drawn dimly, shutting out the new day. He climbed into bed and Mickey rolled over, saying, "I've been waiting for you all night. Where have you been?"

He jumped, surprised at her presence in his bed.

"Jesus, girl, you scared the hell out of me. Where's your truck?"

"In the shed. I wanted to surprise you when you got back."

"You sure did that, but you're definitely what I need right now." He rolled next to her and took her in his arms, pushing the length of his body against her warm suppleness.

"Judging from the smell of whiskey, my guess is you stayed at Elmer's. Am I right or am I not?"

"Dead right. Dead, tragically, hungover right," he said. And then he told her about the Boykins and she laughed. And when he told her about the cop from Wyoming via Paris, Texas, she laughed some more.

"You sure Elmer didn't hire the guy as a joke? It sounds like something he'd conjure up to make your day."

"That's always a possibility, but I think not this time. He's too preoccupied with his damn dogs and the burning coal to plan anything like that," said Joe while reaching over for a cigarette on the bedside table.

"One for me, too," Mickey trilled.

He lit both of them, handed one to her, and placed an ashtray between them.

"The whole thing with the cop was weird, but then everything I have to do with cops is a little twisted. They always mess with people. With their heads. Any way they can. A uniform, a gun, and those silly glasses, think they're hot shit and can jerk any of us around whenever they want. I'd have no qualms about wasting one of them. One, hell, a whole bunch of the pricks. I hate them all . . . well, except for Egyptian. He's okay."

"Easy there, big boy," she said in a soft voice. "The last time you talked this way, got on one of your anti-cop, anti-control jags, you poured all that sugar and great Vermont maple syrup in the Drew squad cars. Maybe it was worth it, but at the expense of that wonderful syrup? I think not, Joseph."

Whenever she called him Joseph he knew two things. One, she was worried about him, and two, she wanted to get laid. He didn't like it when she grew frightened or anxious. He did like it when she got "hot," to use her word, so he said, "Just blowing off steam, Mickey. Means nothing."

They smoked in silence, enjoying each other's company and warmth. She stubbed out her smoke, took his and did the same, then she pulled his head down to her breasts and said "There," in a soft husky voice. "Isn't that what you were after when we found that buffalo skull?"

Joe said nothing, preferring instead to suck her nipples and fondle the warm, furry moistness between her legs. She sighed, then moaned and climbed on top of him. When they were finished they both fell back on the now damp bed. Joe got up, opened a window, and turned on the small fan on the floor over by the door. Not even nine and already above eighty degrees. He went out to the kitchen and brought back a pitcher of iced tea and two glasses.

They worked on the cold liquid straight from the pitcher and smoked more cigarettes. Then Mickey turned to him and used her long fingers to arouse him again.

"Jesus, Mickey. You trying to kill me off?"

"I need it this morning. I need your cock inside me." She mounted him once again and began rocking, moaning and fondling her breasts. They continued working toward their climax and when Mickey came, she screamed and looked down at Joe with a glazed, faraway expression and growled, "Bill, I could fuck you all day." Her body shuddered again and she cried out, "Oh God. God," and then collapsed onto Joe's sweaty chest panting. She moaned indistinguishable words.

Joe lay there stunned, wondering about what she'd just said, what she may have revealed. Foxen? Some drunk cowboy in town? His stomach felt like he'd just eaten ground glass. He tried to sit up and dizziness drove him back down. Bill. That's all he could see in his head. He turned his head toward Mickey. She lay on her back with her eyes open, staring at the ceiling, at nothing. She was lost someplace else far away. Maybe with Bill. He wanted to grab her and shake her and yell at her *Who the hell is Bill?* But she was not with him now. Her body was lying next to him, but her head was somewhere else. He managed to sit up. He breathed deeply for a while then stood and staggered naked into the kitchen. He collapsed into a chair at the kitchen table, pulled the bottle of whiskey to him, and started drinking. It was nearly full. The bottles always seemed to be full or maybe they always seemed to be empty. Time passed and the whiskey ripped hotly through him and eased the maniacal fire in his head some.

Bill. Over and over and sordid images rose up within him and wrapped around each other, growing larger and more perverse. Mickey having sex with two men at once while he watched. One behind her and the other beneath her and the scene grew more elaborate and more perverse and the sickness of it aroused him as he sat naked in the chair, and then disgust replaced the arousal. "Fuck this shit. All of it. Goddamnit!" he yelled. He clutched at the whiskey and lit a cigarette. Bill. He felt like he was on the edge of something dark and ugly, the genesis of evil within all of us. Was it Bill Foxen, the son of a bitch from Dark Star he'd heard about? He was old enough to be her father. God, was Mickey that sick? He'd never been close to this place before, had never known what real shock and revulsion could do to someone. He was finding out now. The thought of being with his mother that way flashed into his mind and he shook his head violently and drove the picture away from him. "Jesus!" He drank from the bottle and the booze slopped out of his mouth, down his chin, onto his naked lap.

Mickey slowly came back to herself and the magnitude of what she'd said while in the grip of her ecstasy overwhelmed her.

"God! What have I done?" she said to herself and the empty bedroom while pulling on her jeans and shirt. She knew she'd done something horrible to the man she loved.

She found Joe still sitting naked at the kitchen table with a bottle of Jim Beam in front of him and a smoldering cigarette burning a deep scar into the wood finish. Perspiration was beaded on his forehead. The room stank of cigarette smoke, whiskey, and sweat. He looked up at her with bloodshot eyes and then took a long drink from the bottle. She went out and picked up his jeans in the next room, grabbing his shirt from the floor.

"Put these on, honey," she commanded gently. He did as she asked before slumping back into the chair again.

"How could you . . . Foxen . . . whoever the hell it is," he said in a voice that wasn't his, something that sounded like it was coming from an open grave. He stared at the table for a long time. Mickey waited him out. "Whore. Bitch. Slut." He laughed darkly to himself then fixed her with a stare of hate that tore down through her. "Any names I missed? Hate to shortchange you on this one after all your efforts . . . it's all some damn con isn't it? You screwing Foxen, my old man screwing me, and Dark Star screwing me . . . Well . . . Screw you, too." He laughed morosely, had some more whiskey, dropped his cigarette on the floor, and ground it out with his bare heel. He lit another. "Fucking Foxen. What was I to you, just some asshole to play games with?"

"Joe, the thing with Bill started years ago. It was a mistake," she pleaded. "It's you I want to be with. I know I've lied and done horrible things . . . She began to cry. "I am a bitch and all those other things you said. Goddamnit, I'm sorry to have done this to you and—"

Joe cut her off with another "Fuck you. Listen sweetheart, any other bastard I could probably live with. But Foxen? I don't ever want to see your ass around here again. I'd like to blow your goddamn head off. Get the picture, Mickey dear?" The two were silent. A pair of magpies made up for this gap with a loud argument over something of avian value lying below the big pine over by the shed. Joe looked out the kitchen door and saw another raven sitting atop the tree. "I knew I shouldn't of shot you the other day. Bad luck all the way. What a dumb shit." He drank more bourbon, ground the smoke out with his other heel, and lit another.

"We've all sold our souls," he said.

"That's why we're here Joe," she said. "That's why we're here."

He nodded and went back to the whiskey. Mickey got up and left.

THREE

The five-foot snake struck from its coiled position next to the pile of cement railroad ties that were stacked at the head of the newly laid tracks. The construction worker was conducting his weekly inspection of the ties for cracks that may have occurred when they'd been off-loaded the other day. The rattler's head shot out, its mouth closed, then swiftly it opened wide, the inside white and lined with a dozen or more needlelike teeth. The force of the reptile's unleashed muscles drove the large inward-curving fangs through the man's pants just above the tops of his work boots, sinking the hollow points into the calf muscle, releasing their venom and withdrawing, mouth closed once again, all of this in an instant. The punctures felt like someone had driven a pair of large cactus spines into the worker's flesh and he screamed, stumbled, and fell next to the ties. Several smaller snakes lay coiled in the shadows and they, too, lashed out, razor-sharp fangs piercing the man's arm, his larynx, and his right eye. The rattlers slithered away to the shelter of some crumbling rock nearby. The extreme dose of venom circulated swiftly through the man's body, first causing an overwhelming sense of giddiness like a cheap Benzedrine rush. This was followed by weakness and numbness bordering on paralysis. The bite areas began to swell and turn bright red with smudges of purple. The man, now lying on his side in the dirt, vomited on his arm and hands. His pulse became feeble and thready. His blood pressure plummeted. Within twenty minutes he was dead.

There was no one around to see this happen. He was out here alone making the inspection on a Sunday afternoon, the one day Dark Star employees and various other subcontractors took off. The punching through of the rail line along the Workman was not yet halfway completed and it was already mid-August. The crews were far behind schedule because of two earlier accidents. First two men on the construction crew were killed by a slab of sandstone that sheared from a cliff a few miles back up the tracks. Then the machinery sloughed off into the river when an underground trickle of water became a full-fledged spring and turned the ground around the railbed into quicksand. And cold, blustery weather would be dropping down from northern Canada soon. The worker's body cooled following death as it lay there in the fading orange light of the setting sun. Ants, wasps, and beetles were already at work devouring the man's flesh. They crawled through his mouth, down his throat, and began chewing on his stomach and intestines. Others nibbled and munched through his eyes and bored into his brain. An insect banquet high on the Workman.

Kilduff was on the scene by five thirty-five the next morning, as soon as he got the call from the first crews to show up for work. The body was a mess. The insects had made serious headway overnight, leaving oozing trails in the man's skin. Coyotes had gnawed away at his face and fingers, and apparently a much larger animal had ripped open the dead man's stomach, tearing out the skin and muscles in one large bite. Whatever the animal was, it had left a slimy string of dead man's intestines looped over the pile of cement ties. The pile of guts was already covered with flies. The ropy mess hummed and buzzed an iridescent blue-green as the early-morning light played off the bugs. Huge tracks, the size of both a man's hands pressed into the ground with great force, led across the rocky soil before disappearing at the edge of a sandstone escarpment.

"Jesus," said Kilduff. He had seen his share of gruesome deaths over the years, bodies smashed to pulp by cave-ins, blown apart by explosions, mangled by machinery accidents, but this corpse was the worst. Already beginning to bloat, savaged by the animals and insects, with an expression of abject horror on what was left of the face. Lips chewed away, tobacco-stained teeth opened wide in a grin of agonized death. There was a dried, cloudy yellow discharge from the suppurating wounds caused by the snakes. The eyes were gone, leaving dried, withering sockets. "Never seen anything worse," he said to the men gathered around the body. He turned away, coughed and spit up the morning's coffee, wiped his mouth on a shirt-sleeve and turned back. "Never heard of animals eating a carcass that's been killed by rattlesnakes. When's the damn coroner getting here?"

"He called on his truck phone and said he'd be down from Garland by six-thirty. An ambulance is coming with him."

This was now the third accident. Kilduff was concerned, both for his men and about completing the line before winter. He'd never missed a deadline, but then he'd never had to contend with any of this before. And, god, the size of those tracks. The dog, coyote, whatever, must weigh at least two hundred pounds. He'd seen Irish wolfhounds, Newfoundlands, and Saint Bernards that size, but never coyotes or even wolves. It wasn't possible. The last of the buffalo wolves had been trapped out of this country decades ago, and the way these tracks vanished into nothingness at the base of that rock wall, the situation was like some kind of northern high plains voodoo.

"What the hell gives here?" he wondered.

"How's that, boss?" asked his foreman.

"Oh nothing, Jim. Just thinking out loud." He looked at the other man. "How the guys taking this? Any trouble you see brewing?"

"Couple of 'em puked when they saw the body or what's left of it. Few more grumbled about shit work and bad luck on the job, but that's about it. Nothing I wouldn't expect to hear under the circumstances." The foreman paused and stared at the river flowing muddy and oily a few yards away. "I can handle it, boss. Worked with most of the men over at McCoy and down in Wyoming. They trust me and will do what I say. It's okay."

"Glad to hear it," said Kilduff with a nod. "I've got to get back and call Foxen. Let me know if there are any snags with the coroner." He looked at the river and wondered what was going to happen next. "I'm going to ask Foxen if we can go seven days a week. And I'll work out an incentive bonus for the men, but keep quiet on that for now."

"No problem," said the foreman, but before he could continue, the earsplitting noise of large rocks crashing down the cliff echoed through the river canyon. It sounded like a mortar attack to Kilduff, reminding him of battles he'd barely survived in Vietnam over a quarter century ago.

Boulders the size of garbage cans bounced and crashed off the pile of broken rock at the base of the cliff then caromed into a flatcar loaded with steel rails. The stone exploded like bombs, shards of rock whistling through the air, clanging into the machinery and tearing into the men. Fingers, hands, torsos, and legs were torn into bloody, ragged pieces. It was over in seconds. Men were screaming, moaning, or lying on the ground unconscious or dead. It looked like a combat zone. Yellow-green dust filled the air.

Kilduff's left arm was bleeding, the skin ripped just below the elbow by a sharp hunk of rock. His foreman was lying on the ground at his feet, blood bubbling around the edges of a spear-shaped piece of stone embedded in his skull. Others staggered around bleeding, clothes shredded, in shock. The ones who weren't hurt either ran to help their injured comrades or were fleeing for their lives back up the tracks or leaping into the river and swimming desperately for the opposite bank of the Workman River.

Kilduff raced over to his truck, punched in 911, and yelled, "There's been a major accident on the Workman rail project, mile thirty-six. Men have been killed or are seriously injured. Send every ambulance and emergency vehicle you've got."

"This is the Drew nine-one-one emergency line. Can you repeat the location and nature of the injuries?" a flat voice over the phone asked.

"Men are dead at mile thirty-six on the Workman rail project, goddamnit! Send motherfucking help now. Right now." Kilduff screamed into the receiver.

He looked around. Wounded men, comatose men, dead men were scattered about the work site, bodies draped and slumped at grotesque angles. Wails of pain and terror sliced through the air. Kilduff thought he could taste the salty, metallic flavor of blood on his tongue along with the dusty, gritty feel of slate and sandstone. The railcar had been knocked off the tracks and was resting on its side. The rails were scattered down the bank. Some were partially submerged in the greasy brown water. He looked up at the place where the boulders had come from. Nothing. No sign of anyone or anything that might have caused all this. He followed the avalanche's course down the cliff, bright scrapes and impact marks scarred the five-hundred-foot rock face that consisted of striations of slate, coal, clinker, and sandstone.

Several hundred feet above the top of the cliff, three ravens glided on the morning breeze, riding the air toward the distant

Sanders Mountains that flashed purple, coral, and white in the angled light of the rising sun.

Above the cries of his men's agony, Kilduff thought he heard sounds of laughter coming from beyond the edge of the escarpment. Mad, insane voices that drifted just barely into his hearing, then vanished, then flickered back to him again. Inhuman sounds. Weird. Or perhaps it was only a distant pack of coyotes barking and howling. Could be grasshoppers clacking through the warming air. Then again, maybe it was the wind talking through the grass. The morning breeze died away and with it the laughter.

The ravens cackled as they flew over the devastation below them.

Cruck, cruck, cruck.

They soared on wide, black wings over the cliff across the river, becoming smaller and smaller shapes, dark pinpoints against the blue. Then they were gone.

Joe bounced around on the padded, spring-loaded seat of the old John Deere tractor that had done the field work on the ranch for more years than he could remember. He'd picked the machine up for a song in Ekalaka one day while over there hunting pheasants not far from the Chalk Buttes. The machine was sitting out in front of a service station with a FOR SALE sign on it. He had paid $625, then driven home, hooked up his trailer, and lugged the thing back to the ranch. Since then the dependable machine had plowed fields for wheat, cut hay, pulled stumps, spread manure, and, as it was doing on this hot, blue-sky morning, pulled a baler that was almost as old as itself and literally held together with baling wire. The whole works rattled, wheezed, and clattered over the rough ground. Occasional puffs of blue-black smoke belched from the exhaust, an indication that the engine needed another ring job. One more winter maintenance chore. Clouds of grasshoppers flew up in front of the tractor like crested water alongside the bow of a cruise ship slicing through the ocean. The hoppers flew past Joe in a steady stream, bounced off his face and arms, and sailed by the baler. He worked back and forth in a steady rhythm across the hundred-plus-acre field that ran along the base of a limestone bluff on one side and a small but steady stream that wound around the rest of the perimeter. The added moisture from the creek made this the best hay-producing land Joe had. He counted on this hay to help get his cows through the long winters. Sometimes, in what passed for moist years on the Workman, he got three cuttings, though the third was always a bit on the slim side. This year looked like two, Joe thought, as he watched the rectangular bales spew from the rear of the baler every ten yards and land in the stubble.

As Joe and the machinery droned up and down the field in the growing heat, a slight movement in the trees along the base of the limestone cliff caught his eye. At first he figured it was a mule deer working toward a cut in the rock; then he figured it was one of Coaker's mastiffs because of the animal's short legs. He caught one more ghosting flash of it, noticed a long, bushy tail and that the overall color of the creature was a gray-buff. Not a mastiff with that tail and shading, he thought. He wiped his eyes on his shirtsleeve and looked again. Nothing. Whatever he'd seen was gone.

"Probably one of Coaker's dogs," he said to himself. "Damn heat's playing tricks with my eyes." He continued baling hay.

Through his telescope, Elmer could see two large pipes pouring water into the jagged tear in the baked ground and down onto the burning coal, the place not far from where the Dark Star truck had been swallowed whole the previous spring. The pipes were twelve inches in diameter. They delivered thousands of gallons per minute that gushed and sprayed onto the inferno. Sooty steam shot far above the land, the vaporized liquid billowing from the fissure in whirling, hissing clouds. The crew had been pumping this water into the crack in the earth for three days now with some results. They worked continually. At night beneath the billion stars, huge arc lights illuminated the scene with surreal intensity, the harsh white light throwing long, black, almost alien shapes that mirrored the actions of the men as they went about their business. Nothing like this shadow play had ever been seen on the plateau before. Every twenty-four hours they moved the pipes a hundred feet along the fault, believing that they'd put out a section of the red-hot coal, but Elmer doubted if the seams were any more than temporarily cooled down, waiting to flare up once again as the bituminous coal dried in the intense heat of the adjacent flames and embers. A downdraft of oxygen, a spark or two, and wham, things would be back to the usual simmering, smoking, belching routine.

"Damn fools never will get the thing out," he muttered to the Boykins, which were either sitting next to him or lying supinely on the ground, paws splayed, bellies taking in the noon sun. "Tore all hell out of Joe's place putting in that god-damn well and haul road and for what? A dumb-ass steam bath. Fools, every one of them, I tell ya. All that water those idiots are usin' will make Joe rich yet." Oakley wagged her tail and yowled in agreement. Elmer and the Boykins were on speaking terms once again following the night with Joe that featured the lone wolf's howl. No more silent treatment from his spaniels. No more military rigidity. The dogs were their normal, undisciplined selves again and Elmer, though he'd never admit to this, was relieved. He'd secretly feared that his Boykins' silent treatment would finally wear him out and that he'd have to admit as much to them, a humiliation he was not prepared to face.

Elmer hadn't seen Joe in a while, ever since this latest disaster along the Workman rail line. Graves had pulled up in a cloud of dust as soon as he'd found out about the accident and given Elmer the lowdown before saying he had to run to Miles City to pick up some supplies, fencing material, window screening, and, of course, a few cases of Jim Beam. He promised to get a few boxes of cigars for Elmer at the smoke shop down on Main. That was a week ago. Elmer figured Joe was holed up at Chambers Point shooting his guns, drinking whiskey, and swearing at the sky. Letting off steam, just like the land was out by those big pipes.

Three men died in the avalanche by the river. Several more had been badly injured. One man lost a leg. Another had his spinal cord severed and would be paralyzed for life, and still another was blinded by the shale shrapnel. But the track laying went on, now seven days a week around the clock.

"Serves the dipshits right," Elmer said to Oakley, who blinked her yellow eyes in agreement. "Don't like to see people hurt, but they're messing with our land and our way of life." Oakley barked once. The other dogs turned their heads or rolled over and looked in her direction.

Dark Star and Kilduff had gone out of their way to route the haul road from Elmer's conflagration to the Workman as far from Graves's place as possible. Aside from the fact that this turned out to be the most cost-efficient location, Kilduff wanted to keep as much distance from Joe's raging path as possible. He figured Joe was on a long-term, slow burn that could ignite at any moment at the slightest provocation. Gunfire and worse was entirely possible the way Kilduff saw things. They'd even placed the well far behind a thick stand of Utah juniper back down a hill and out of sight of the house. Not the best location, but workable. The twin pipes ran parallel to the graveled road, and the noise from the huge trucks moving and dumping aggregate to beef up the byway vibrated for miles across the open sage flats and brushy coulees. No more peaceful, silent nights. No more game, either. The muleys and whitetails had vanished, as had the sage grouse and turkeys. Dark Star had completed all of this work in less than a month—the road, the well and pumping station, and the pipelines.

The well tapped into the aquifer, which probably contained billions of gallons of water that had trickled and filtered down through the porous ground over thousands of years—rain, sleet, snowmelt—and was now being wasted away on an unstoppable subterranean fire. The aquifer fed the hundreds of springs that trickled and poured life-giving water out across the plateau. When it was used up, thousands of acres of the country would turn barren, lifeless. The only good thing, if that was indeed the proper word, was the fact that Joe's trout stream was still flowing, perhaps even a little stronger than before the drilling. Joe told Elmer before he left for Miles City that his brown trout were doing fine, but that "the savages had ruined the lower mile of the creek when they put in the haul road." Culverts, mud and rock, oil spills, the works. But the hyperstrain of brown trout had come through the ordeal like pros. The majority of the fish had moved into the upper stretch by Joe's house when the construction began. That mile or so of willow-and alder-lined stream probably had three thousand trout swimming around and nudging each other for prime holding areas and scrambling for every mayfly, caddis, and grasshopper in sight. The incredible number of fish probably made it "one of the finest trout waters in Montana," said Joe, with a wry grin and a flip of the finger toward McCoy and the Consortium's headquarters.

One of the many downsides to all of the construction was the sound of the industrial pump running night and day, a constant visceral drone that wiped out the awesome stillness of the land. Elmer hated the noise and had caught himself more than once clutching one of his hunting rifles, or his .357, or even found himself sighting in through one of his rifle scopes on a member of the water crew. He usually did this at night, when things seemed more intriguing to his mind. "Sort of like jack-lighting deer," he'd whisper to the dogs.

But soon enough he'd pull off the rifle.

"No way, Elmer, you old fart," he'd growl to himself. "Not yet anyway." He was having a high old time smoking his cigars and drinking whiskey while observing the futile efforts of what he liked to call "those numb-nut bastards from the Consortium." Elmer liked the way the word *consortium* rolled around in his mouth. "Consortium. Consortium. Consortium," he'd singsong to some nameless tune of his own creation.

Elmer took a slug of whiskey and a big puff on his cheap green cigar then turned back to the telescope just in time to see men running away from the steaming rip in the ground. He adjusted the focus and zeroed in on the crack, which was rapidly growing wider. Large sheets and chunks of earth sliding into the now gaping hole as if they were being funneled into the maw on a gigantic conveyor. Steam and thick smoke obscured the men as they piled in their black trucks and tore away from the death trap in reverse, wheels spinning as they tried to gain purchase on the loose, sandy ground. Chunks of dead sage and cactus plants spun beneath the burning tires and got tangled in drivetrains, exhaust systems, and axles. The wind carried sounds of the crew screaming and swearing, the human noise distorted and feathered by distance, and Elmer could smell the smoking tires and burning clutches, acrid, greasy scents.

Then an explosion rocked the area with a force that rippled across the land, the concussion of the blast wave knocked Elmer off his feet, blew his hat from his head, and thoroughly upset the sixteen Boykins, which began howling and barking at everything in general while running and leaping in frantic circles. The ground actually rose in a humping wave a couple of feet high, rocking his home and busting out most of the windows. The back door was wrenched from its hinges.

Elmer struggled to his feet and what he saw—well, he didn't need a telescope to view the intense orange fireball unfolding more than a thousand feet above him. Pieces of rock and dirt began raining down on Elmer and the dogs, pounding on his metal silo in sharp pings and loud bangs. A fine dark gray ash started falling down on all of them like perverted snow. The Boykins yipped and snapped as some of the rocks nailed them. They looked up angrily at the sky and howled, eyes flashing with anger at the unexplained attack.

"I could of told 'em, the dumb shits," Elmer lectured to the whirling spaniels. A rock the size of a marble bounced off his head. "Ow. That bastard hurt," he yelled, as he rubbed the spot of impact. "That coal can't be put out by men and their machines. Most likely a ton of flammable gas mixed in that big ol' hole, too. I bet one good goddamn dollar that the shit reignited all at once and went *Kaplooee*. That's all she wrote. Good damn night, Irene."

He set up the telescope, also knocked over by the blast, readjusted the focus, and searched for the Dark Star trucks. He spotted two of them three miles away weaving and sliding up the haul road on the far side of Mad Woman Gulch. The pickups were running at a dangerous speed, a thick cloud of red dust trailing behind. He scanned the horizon for the other truck. Nothing. Then he panned near the source of the still-climbing mushroom cloud. The hole in the ground was now as wide as a football field. Sparks, flames, ash, rocks, sage brush, weathered juniper, long-dead ponderosa stumps and limbs, all sorts of stuff were soaring into the air like some berserk fountain. Swinging the scope slowly to his left, he picked out the other wrecked pickup more than one hundred yards from the blast site. Nose-down and crumpled like an accordion, windshield and all the other glass smashed out. The explosion must have heaved the truck a couple of hundred feet in the air before it crashed into the parched, rock-hard soil nose-first. Elmer zeroed in on the cab, at least what he could see of it. A bloody mess. Both men were decapitated, their severed heads resting on the ground in front of the mangled hood. The old man almost threw up, but a pull of whiskey controlled the situation.

"Hell of a bad way to go," he said to Oakley, now standing next to him. The other dogs were arranged in their customary semicircle behind them. "Hell of a way to die."

The man and his dogs stared out across the fiery Workman Plateau and watched as the mushroom cloud kept rising.

The evening of the explosion, Kilduff dialed Foxen down in Denver. It seemed like all he'd been doing for the past couple of weeks was talking with his boss. The first two deaths along the rail line, the damaged equipment, the man killed by the rattlesnake, then the three others, and now this. The damn media was all over the story, hanging around the bars and restaurants in Drew, outside the McCoy work site, the Workman River site, and on the fringes of the Yoter place. Several reporters and cameramen had tried to approach the old man, but he'd driven them away with rifle and pistol fire, not to mention that pack of dogs of his. Dragged down one guy from CNN. Let him go and turned on his camera.

Kilduff got Foxen's secretary, whom he knew well, and filled her in briefly on the situation while she tracked down her boss on another line.

"What a zoo Yoter's got going. Hell, what a zoo I've got going. We need to pull off this job right now. Drop the whole thing. Make a big environmental sob-story pitch and cut our losses. We're losing men, and I can't stand that. Never had that happen before. And we're millions of dollars over budget already. Yoter's coal is a damn sinkhole. Hope the old man goes for jumping ship on this one. Always listened to me in the past. He damn well better this time."

"He might," she said. "But I've never seen him this worked up or focused before. He's on the line now. Good luck." One connection died and another clicked to life.

"Pete. I already got the news. It's been flashed on network TV," said Foxen in a loud, angry voice. "Saw it on CNN. Jesus, those dogs did a number on that camera guy. What in the name of hell you boys got goin' up there?"

Kilduff filled him in on the latest tragedy; that even though there had been a feel of sabotage to some of the mayhem, there was no sign of outside interference. Kilduff also informed Foxen that six of his best men had quit not only the job, but Dark Star completely, and more were threatening to do the same. That environmental groups were starting to get their poor, febrile little imaginations all worked up. He went on to describe his ideas on how Dark Star could pull out of this without any further damage, maybe even get some good PR. Donate money to the various environmental groups in the region, set up trust funds for the dead men's families, and clean up the haul road and Workman River.

"No way!" yelled Foxen. Kilduff held the receiver away from his ear. "We never quit on a course of action we've already begun, that we're committed to. That's policy. Carved in stone. No way. The trust funds—yes. The other shit—never!"

"But Bill . . ." Kilduff started.

"No. Period. Got it?"

"Yes, but it's a mistake."

"Screw the mistakes, Pete. I'll fly up there in the morning and we'll straighten things out.

"See you at the airport."

The line went dead with a loud *click*.

Kilduff looked at the phone and wondered what would happen next.

"We're all going to be screwed major on this one," he said to no one but himself.

He stood up and looked out the window to the Workman Plateau simmering under the brutal August sun, which seemed to hang motionless in a cloudless sky burned from blue to a searing white. Miles away he could see coal smoke drifting across the barren, burned-out land on Yoter's place.

"I can feel it. We're history," he said to the view stretched out before him.

Coaker Triplett's two mastiffs were on the trail of a crippled mule deer. The pair had probably run down more game on the Workman than Joe, Elmer, and Coaker had shot in their lifetimes. Most of the area's residents considered the dogs a menace, and both dogs had the scars along their flanks from buckshot and bullets to prove it. The dogs weighed more than two hundred pounds each. They'd drop their squared heads down to the ground to check the scent of the deer, the dogs' large, drooping ears dragging in the dust. And then off they'd go again, thick paws pounding the ground as they loped along, relentlessly closing distance on their prey, an animal with three good legs and one badly mangled one that had been tangled and then torn in some discarded, rusty barbed wire from a fence Dark Star had ripped up while laying the haul road. The mastiffs came up over a small hill and spotted the panicked deer hobbling down a steep cut on the edge of Mad Woman Gulch. The muley was desperately trying to reach the sheltering tangle of brush and grass at the bottom of the coulee. The buck knew its way through the tight, tunnel-like game trails that wound back and forth along the bottom of the gulch. The dogs broke into a run, saliva dripping from the corners of their mouths, big white teeth glinting in the sun. The deer stumbled over an exposed tree root, lost its footing, and rolled up against the gray hulk of a dead ponderosa. The animal struggled to regain its feet. The mastiffs, jaws agape, lunged for the throat and exposed belly of the deer.

Neither of the killers reached its prey.

Something as large as the two mastiffs combined roared as it leapt from its vantage point on top of a flat outcropping of sandstone above the deer. The creature flew down the slope, covering the forty feet between the rock and the dogs in one bound. The lone wolf had been tracking Coaker's hounds for a week now, always keeping the breeze at the right angle so that the mastiffs never winded the large carnivore. The wolf crashed into one of the mastiffs, driving it into the other. Both dogs were knocked down to the bottom of the gulch. The wolf was right behind them. As soon as it regained its balance, the predator nearly tore the head off one mastiff with a powerful swipe of its huge teeth, then swung on the other and ripped its belly open from hind legs to chest. Both Coaker's dogs lay on the ground, blood splattered all over the brush and ground, pooled beneath the bodies. The disemboweled mastiff weakly lifted its head, life's light fading from its brown eyes. It tried to lick at the tear in its belly but died while doing so, the heavy head falling back in the dirt with a thump.

The wolf shook itself, rearranging its fur, blood and pieces of guts spraying in a wide arc. The animal looked at the kills, then let loose with the howl of a natural-born killer, a sound that swept up out of Mad Woman Gulch, cut across the Workman Plateau, and roared across the sage flats. The wolf moved to the damaged mule deer, which was now waiting for doom to come its way. Both animals, breathing heavily from their exertions and the presence of death, stared at each other. The wolf approached the deer. The predator crouched low to the ground, then leapt and crashed down on the head of the frightened animal, breaking its neck. The wolf began tearing away chunks of the dead deer's flesh.

From its vantage point on a tree limb thirty feet above the place of the ambush, a small puma watched the curious drama. The smell of blood and killing was thick in its nostrils. The fur on the cat's back stood up. The puma had also been tracking the deer, but was keeping well away from the mastiffs. When the wolf was gone, the panther dropped to the ground and pounced on the deer, ripping out its jugular. The cat tore at the still-warm fleshy remains, eating its fill before dragging the mangled carcass into the brush. The kill was covered with grass, sticks, and dirt. The cat marked the place with its urine, a warning to other animals to keep away. Then the puma climbed back up to its limb, cleaned itself, and dozed in the heat of the day.

Joe and Elmer set out from Elmer's place before sunrise, at four A.M. They were in the old flatbed with the dogs, four in the front, two of those on Joe's lap, and twelve on the bed; it was still dark out, stars glowing above with the Milky Way still showing as a luminous band arcing the sky and the last of the moon dropping down behind them over the Sanders. They were off to mend some fence. This section was stitched and stretched along a ragged three-mile line of weathered juniper posts that climbed and dipped among the native grasses, wiry sagebrush, and prickly pear cactus. Elmer had not been over to this part of his land in years, but he seemed to remember that the last time, when he was out "Chasing all hell and back after the damn grouse," the barbed wire was rusting "pretty damn bad" and sagging "like my god-almighty-awful jowls." The drive to the work coursed along a red gravel road that turned into a dirt-and-rock two-track. They crawled and bounced about a dozen miles up over bluffs, around enormous piles of eroding sandstone that looked like Egyptian monuments, and then a last run across a flat of "some of the finest damn grass in the West" according to Elmer. He'd purchased another fifty longhorns from a breeder up near Sweetgrass just south of the Alberta border, and the cows were due in next week. He wanted them to fatten up and adjust to their new surroundings in this grass, but that old fence line needed looking after. Elmer would never sell the cows. He was in love with the romanticism of having the Texas longhorns roaming his land. He didn't need money, just an excuse to keep busy at this late stage of his life. Joe and Elmer would knock that work out today with steady, uninterrupted motion. Replace rotten posts with new steel ones. Pull up and tighten sagging strands of wire. Replace broken stretches and so on until the task was done. They'd worked together doing things like this hundreds of times over the years on both of their places. Fence lines, branding, neutering, haying, new barn roofs, all the dirty hard labor of their lives. Elmer had loaded up the truck with spools of wire, stakes, stretching equipment, coolers full of food, beer, and plenty of water for all of them, including the dogs. Even in the dim light the temperature was already above sixty and appeared anxious to reach ninety by noon. As they approached a gate in the line, the day was fast turning from purpled dark to silver to yellow-gold seemingly all at once across the east. Bands of bloodred and pink-orange light flickered just above the horizon.

Elmer shut down the rig, the engine slowly coming to a stop in a series of pops, smoky belches, and a final rattling, shimmying shiver that ended in the old engine wheezing into silence. Joe hopped out and headed for the gate where they'd pass through to run the line. The gate was a cobbled mess consisting of four strips of the wire attached to four posts and hooked to a pole sunk into the ground. There were probably a million of these in this country, and Joe often thought he'd opened every damn one of them. He had the scars from the mean wire biting through his gloves to prove his point. Pulling on his gloves, he pushed on the fence for slack, pulled off the holding band, and dragged the gate out of the way.

"Wire's not too bad, at least here, anyway. Those creosote posts of years ago seem to be holding up okay, too," said Joe. "We'll kick this one in the ass by noon." He was about to say more when a canine howl of enormous and now seemingly elliptical dimensions echoed across the lightening land, a sound so loud, so ancient, even the breeze checked itself and died down into the rough grass. Oakley and the rest of the dogs stopped dead. They'd been sniffing around a very dead and very dried-up antelope carcass over by the fence. Each dog sat down on its haunches and looked off to the east in the direction of a wind-carved bluff that looked something like the head of a beaver, rounded skull and slightly lower snout defined by eroded seams of sandstone and clinker. The sound came from over there.

The day grew lighter and hotter by the minute. The unearthly howl took forever to dissipate in the still air, and when it was gone the land was without sound. Small birds ceased their chirping. Hawks and eagles were somewhere else now. A band of mule deer browsing a few hundred yards away when the men had first arrived were nowhere to be seen. Even the millions of grasshoppers were silent. It was as if that ungodly howl had pierced the soul of this country and purged it of any pretensions to life.

Joe just stared until Elmer said, "A goddamn buffalo wolf, I'll bet my last pint of whiskey on it." He pulled one from a pants pocket, took a deep swallow, and lobbed it to Joe, who did the same. "Yeah, damn straight it's coming, all damn hell of it. Weather, fire, darkness. God only knows what the hell else, and He never tells me a damn thing. Let's get to this fence before I expire from the stress of worrying about our little bit of the world."

The two men got down to it. The dogs remained motionless and silent until Oakley stood and slowly walked to the top of a small rise and faced the bluff.

AAAHHRRGhhhh.

The dog listened as the sound returned softened and rearranged from bouncing around the rock and sand. Then Oakley let loose again and again. The dog stared hard at the bluff before finally sitting down to wait for, as Elmer said, "God only knows what."

"Not in all my damn years, not in any single one of the full-tilt, crazy one of them, Joe. Not in all of them. Nothing like this god-blamed stuff of the past few weeks ever happened here. Damn near leaves me at a loss for words, and that ain't a good sign neither."

Joe finished crimping a strand of the biting wire, took off his heavy work gloves, and looked up at Elmer, who was ratcheting a come-along to tighten the fence. He saw that the old man wasn't troubled or scared, just plain amazed and mystified. Joe thought that Elmer had seen and done it all. The Workman proved him wrong.

They finished up the last section a little after noon. Most of the wire and posts would hold for a few more years and didn't require their attention. Some of the stuff was rusted and broken. A few posts had weathered through. The hard part was sinking the steel post replacements three feet down into the rock-hard ground. They worked a heavy, iron post pounder together, facing each other, grabbing the handles and banging the thing up and down on the tops of the post. The force of the effort slamming off the ground vibrated through their arms. The harsh metallic noise numbed their eardrums until all they heard was the ringing metal inside their heads.

Halfway through the line they came across another long-dead antelope that had died when it failed to clear the top strand of wire and tangled its hind feet. The poor beast's struggles to free itself had only made things worse. The wire was torn loose from the two nearest posts and wrapped tightly around the pronghorn's chest, cutting through the hide and digging into the rib bones. Neither man said a word as they clipped the strands of barbed wire and dragged the animal off into a clump of junipers.

They ate a lunch of antelope steak sandwiches on rye bread and some of Elmer's homemade dill pickles. He used rye bread in the brine to ferment the cucumbers. The yeast did the job. And there was some potato salad spiked with jalapeños and Bermuda onions that Joe had put together the night before. A pair of huge ponderosas provided shade from the sun, but little relief from the heat. They leaned back against the rough, red-rust bark and wound down from the work. The dogs were scattered about them lying on their sides, or on their stomachs with hind legs splayed backward frog-style. They'd consumed about twenty pounds of dog chow and a few gallons of water. Snores, sleepy slobbering sounds, paws twitching in dreams, an ear flicking every now and then, that was it for the dog contingent. Oakley, ever the avant-garde leader, was crashed out some feet from the others, belly basking in the sun, legs cast off at all angles, head lolling to one side, tongue hanging out almost into the grass.

"Damn dog's a piece of work," said Elmer as he worked on a can of cold beer. "Maybe I ought to enter that one in the Westminster Dog Show. Show those sissy-ass poodles a thing or two. Goddamn, you ever see those things when they show that piece-of-shit carnival on TV? Damn embarrassment to dogs the whole wide world. Awful. Just plain and simple awful.

"Now, take my well-heeled pack here. They're all a bunch of loose-lipped idiots, but I love 'em just the same, especially now that their little lame-brained insurrection's over. Hell, they were only acting on what was coming into their dog brains.

Couldn't help themselves, the poor suckers." He started to say some more, but caught himself and instead pulled out another can of beer buried in the ice in a cooler he was using as an armrest. Elmer shook it up with a violent up-and-down motion, popped the tab, and shot a spray at Oakley, who only opened one eye, grunted, and went back to sleep. "That wolf, the weather that's coming, Dark Star, the whole goddamn bunch of it has those dogs sorely perplexed."

"Thanks for stopping before you got to the part about me and Mickey screwing on the side of the road. You know about all this bullshit with her?" Elmer nodded. "Don't know if I'll ever come to terms with all of it. Cuts through my guts. Makes me feel lost." Joe stopped, shook his head, then looked at Elmer. "How'd you know?"

"Don't worry on that situation, Joseph. Time will take care of that. Hell, what's one more damn scar. Between us we got a shed full. Just keep pushing, grinding out the fucking days. You got no choice in the matter and you aren't the chickenshit suicide kind. Here"—he tossed a fresh pint of bourbon to Joe—"this works for me and I'm way too old to worry about those fools who think I've got a drinking problem. Hell yes I do. Had one all my life. Can't imagine life without whiskey or these genuine, made-in-Detroit cigars, either for that matter. Fuck 'em."

"Yeah, thanks for the sage wisdom, but answer my question. How did you know about Mickey and me . . . and Foxen?" said Joe. "I never said a damn thing to you."

"Live long enough and you get pretty damn good at reading people and putting two and two together. It isn't brain surgery when you come moping around my place and head straight for the whiskey bottle. What else does that to a man? Missing a shot on a bird? A flat tire? Hell, I admit that the cheese has slipped off my cracker. That I'm a few bricks shy of a full load, and I don't have both oars in the water, either, but I can figure out a few things. I'm not that out of it."

"We're all out of it, Elmer," said Joe, but he was smiling a bit now. "Just crazy and senseless, but when I think on that, hell, when I think about it, maybe my life's been insane for a long time."

"Well, goddamn, the boy's finally figured this little out-of-tune ditty out. 'Course it's insane. The whole damn premise is built on our half-ass notions of what the world is. Crazy damn shit that is. But I know what you mean. I've been off my fine-tuned natural rhythm ever since I sold the mineral rights to Dark Star. Lost my edge. Can't even swear like an old rancher's supposed to anymore." He finished his beer and opened another. "Dark Star, you, me, we haven't done right by this country. Oh, we all got our lame-dick reasons and excuses. The country needs energy. I need the money. I care for the land. I've lived here all my life. What a load of horseshit. Tearing that coal out. My letting the bastards do it all the damn while kidding myself that it was a pissing joke and they'd never get away with any of it. Hell, I don't need the money. I got more than I'll ever need." He paused to light the stub of cigar wedged in a corner of his mouth. "That dead antelope. My fence killed it. Nothing else. Who in the Sam hell am I kidding? Not the land. It knows better. I can't explain this to you buddy, but the land knows, more than us, and we feel it but damn well choose to ignore the truth. The dogs really feel it. And that huge, big-ass wolf is here to make sure we get the point."

Joe lit a smoke.

"No one's ever seen that wolf, Elmer. Probably just the way the wind works through the rock."

Elmer stared hard at Joe.

"Just when I start to think that your half-ass pea brain may actually hold a thought or two, you prove me dead wrong, Joseph. Damn, face the truth out here. At least some of it before you die an ignorant fool. We all think we're so fucking smart. So hip, to use one of your crazy jazz horn blowers' terms. Horrible music. Simply horrible. Sounds like someone's strangling a rabid otter. God almighty. Art my ass."

He took a puff on the cigar and a swig of beer.

"We don't know diddly about the natural world, about what we call home or our land. Not shit for shinola. If we could ever drop our lame-ass egos and admit that we're plain, shit-for-brains stupid, we'd know a hell of a lot more, but enough of this crap. I brought my Winchester pump. Barrels bent some but it shoots and I tossed in the Wingmaster for you. Let's see if these worthless pieces of canine shit can hunt. Shells and guns are in the tool chest. Help an old man out. I got another beer and another sip of this real high-class whiskey to attend to."

"Damn Elmer, you surprise the hell out of me sometimes."

"Don't start with that shit now. I'm no genius, but I'm vaguely aware of some of the bullshit that goes on around here. Jesus damn Christ. The boy thinks I'm an idiot. You dogs hear that. Well get off your dead butts and lets roust some birds. About eight or ten would be real good burned all to hell on the grill the way that man over there does it. Fucking pyromaniac to my way of thinking. Come on now. Up, all of you mongrel jokes. Get up."

Elmer was standing now, reaching for the shotgun Joe was handing him. All sixteen Boykins were up and circling the two men. Hopping in the air and creating a mad din filled with barks, excited coughs, and moans. Sixteen tails wagging like crazy. Oakley was whining, groaning, and laughing all at once, sparks flying from those amber eyes. The game was afoot and all of them were ready.

"Prettiest damn noise on earth. Lot better than that jazz shit of yours. Give me these slaphappy dogs wailing away out here any time."

The day was really hot now. Finding birds on a blue-sky afternoon like this one would be tough. They hiked over a ridge and dropped down into a brushy draw that held the dying remains of a small spring and some shade. A few striped chorus frogs croaked away as they approached, but the sound stopped when the dogs began working the bushes. Midges and electric-blue damselflies buzzed above small pockets of still water puddled up in depressions in the rocky streambed. Leeches and small larvae wriggled through the bright green scum on the edges of this water. The dogs scoured the cover, routing under clumps of juniper, nosing through the grass, around brushy piles of rock, everywhere. They were intent on their task, looking back every now and then to see where the two men were, sometimes waiting on them to catch up.

They walked down the drainage without the dogs turning birdy once. The place seemed lifeless from a grouse standpoint. The wind flowed through the tops of the old pines in a soft, lonely sigh. They walked across a grass-and-sage flat to another draw that opened where a large stand of ponderosas began. No water showing here. Just a few moist spots in the dark, grassy, shaded reaches.

"We'll push up this mother, then work across the flat above," said Elmer. "Always some sharps on top crunching the crickets. We'll get our supper."

This draw was more of the first. A few insects, scattered patches of shade, and lots of heat. Joe was sweating when they broke loose out on the open flat. The afternoon breeze ran warm but cooled him all the same. He looked over at Elmer. The old guy was dry as a bone and breathing normally, like he'd been sitting in his porch rocker for the past two hours.

"Joe, have a bite of this and wash it down with the water while I attend to the dogs." He tossed him the bourbon.

Elmer pulled a two-gallon jug from his canvas rucksack, kneeled down, and poured the water in a bowl he'd brought for this purpose. The Boykins lined up in single file led by

Oakley and drank their fill. He drained the one jug and pulled out another.

"Polite bunch of miscreant farts, aren't they. Yeah, you're all a bunch of good ones, and I forgive you the past weeks' foolishness. Good dogs. Let's hunt up some grouse so we can watch Joe put on one of his famous shooting displays. Keep your tails low, he's a ground-sluicer at heart."

Elmer looked over at Joe and laughed, a sound a lot like Oakley's bark.

"Glad to be rid of the water. Thirty damn pounds weighs hard on an old man's back. Crickets are here, so are the birds. Be alert, Joe."

The crickets were everywhere. Crawling and hopping at Joe's feet. Big black ones the size of Milk Duds. They began to work through the knee-high, golden dry grass, the dogs swinging back and forth about twenty yards in front of them.

Then Oakley stopped dead, as if someone had frozen the spaniel in time. The dog's body was stretched like an arrow pointing at a large clump of sage and dense grass. Front right paw curled up, tail straight and slightly angled to the sky. The other dogs went motionless, honoring their leader's point.

"Get ready Joe. She's gonna bust loose any second."

The two men moved forward slowly, walking like the ground was littered with eggshells, shotguns in the ready position. Then, sounding like a helicopter gone mad, half a dozen sage grouse, big ones, seven or eight pounds each, whomped up out of the sage, wings beating frantically. Squawking and clucking in alarm as only the big grouse can. As soon as they got up above the cover they cut with the breeze and began to sail away. Elmer dropped one on a swinging shot to the left and another as it raced downwind. Both birds crumpled then smacked into the ground, feathers everywhere. Joe missed one in front of him, then nailed another about forty yards out. All of this seemed like it was happening at once—brown, tan, gray feathers and beating wings, gunfire, smoke, leaping and barking dogs, brown fur racing everywhere. The dogs broke off into three groups and ran down the birds. Oakley was in the lead and went after Joe's. When the Boykin tried to retrieve the sage hen, the bird turned out to be quite alive though one wing was broken. The grouse stood its ground then leapt at Oakley, who in turn hopped straight up off the ground and pounced on the bird, snapping its neck in one swipe of her jaws.

"Damn sure as hell wouldn't want that one mad at me," said Elmer. His face was flushed with the thrill of shooting and the rush of killing. Joe was the same. "Goddamn I love this shit," said Elmer. Then he let out a deep bass howl that carried far across the Workman. The dogs looked at their leader and did the same. The land vibrated with the energy. All here was as it should be again. Wild, alive.

"Christ, beat-it-all-to-hell, Joe. Now we're living. Damn sage hens aren't the best eating, but I'm sure you'll find a work-around on that one. Thought we'd scare up the sharps. Didn't figure on the sage hens being here for a few more weeks yet. Here, take a pull on this and have one of these fine cigars."

"When I'm done with those birds, they'll taste damn good, Elmer. Count on it."

The dogs were in a semicircle around the two, a pair of sage hens dropped on the ground between them. Oakley pushed through the pack, dragging a bird that must have weighed in at ten pounds. She released the grouse right on top of Elmer's boots, looked up, and barked a little tune that seemed to say, *We're in tall grass now, boss.* Elmer bent over and rubbed her ears.

"Fine work there, Oakley. Goes for the rest of you hounds, too. Damn fine dog work. You done your breed proud and warmed a crazy old bastard's heart. Yeah we're in tall grass and we're living damn large this here moment."

The two men lit up; the cheap cigars, now quite dry from the day's heat and nonexistent humidity, torched in a cloud of smoke. They worked on the whiskey and laughed out loud. "Life is good, Joe. Tough as hell. A mean son of a bitch, but don't this beat all? Real hunting dogs. World-class cigars. Smooth whiskey and all of this."

Elmer held his shotgun out away from him and swung it back and forth to take in the Workman blazing away all around them.

He was on his hands and knees hiding behind a small clump of willows, peering into the water while dozens of his brown trout gorged on caddisfly nymphs as the little worms wriggled their way up to the surface to emerge as fluttering gray helicopters.

The brown trout flashed copper and bronze as they twisted and turned this way and that chasing the caddis. Joe could see the white of their mouths as they opened and closed. And he could see their crimson and black spots as the fish twisted their bodies to snare the food. One brown in particular caught his attention. A trophy by this stream's standards. Eleven, twelve inches. The fish held on the bottom near the far bank as a small slip of current pushed the nymphs directly to him. Only minor flickerings of its tail and fins were necessary to hold position as the brown sucked in the insects. Suddenly from beneath an undercut grassy bank a few feet downstream from the big brown a fat, bright orange submarine emerged, ponderously working its way upstream. Joe stared through the water as the twenty-inch fish nosed among the streambed cobble, kicking up the nymphs with little bursts of sand. The creature appeared to be a giant goldfish. *Koi,* he thought as he picked up his bamboo rod and dropped a short cast several feet in front of the behemoth. The fish had washed through the dam from the reservoir and found its way through Dark Star's sludge and up his creek, Joe figured. The Drew locals would drop near anything in there. Goldfish, muskies, salmon, even jellyfish. His weighted Hare's Ear nymph, a pattern of tan feathers and fur, sank to the bottom right in line with the course of the koi. Joe twitched the fly with a slight tug on his line, and the fish surged up to it and took. Joe drove the hook's barb home by sharply lifting up the rod, hanging on as the intruder surged all over the small pool scattering terrified brown trout in all directions. The trout fled in a flurry of miniature wakes and sparkling splashings. The koi must have weighed close to three pounds; the lightweight fly rod was bent in an exaggerated U shape. Back and forth the fish went, pulling powerfully. Joe hoped his slender leader would hold and that his fine rod would not splinter under the strain. The tug-of-war went on for twenty minutes. The bottom of the pool was cloudy from the fine sand stirred up by the koi. Joe stood next to the bank now. The fish swam in small circles and listed to one side. He pulled it to the bank and to the surface. The koi was exhausted, gills flapping open and closed. It rolled over on its belly and Joe bent down and snatched it by the tail, lifting it far above his trout stream in a spray of water. The iridescent oranges and yellows of the koi glistened in the sun. A glowing presence that somehow had found its way from someone's aquarium all the way up to the Workman Plateau. Quite a journey. A beautiful fish.

"Where did you come from?" Joe asked, as he moved his head right up to the koi's, whose thick, rubbery lips puckered and unpuckered. The eyes of the fish seemed to look through him without any hint of awareness or comprehension of the difficult spot it was now in, hanging upside down in the hot breeze and several feet from the safety of the cool water bur- bling beneath its head. "Maybe from Paris, Texas." Joe laughed. "I hope not."

He got down on his knees and placed the koi back in the stream. The brown trout scattered at this intrusion into their cold, clear world, but soon they returned and watched from a distance, their bodies quivering with fear and curiosity. Joe moved the fish slowly back and forth in the current. The well-oxygenated water slowly brought it back to life, and with a pulse of its tail the koi swam free. Joe watched as the orange fish resumed feeding on the caddis nymphs.

"Where did you come from?" he asked again. "Where does any of this come from?"

He stood there for hours staring at his brown trout as they fed, now on the surface as the caddis began whirring and swooping above and across the water. The koi disappeared from view somewhere around the bend. The browns just kept sipping the bugs. The late-summer air was dry, but the stream smelled rich, full of life, almost sensual. The sun set in a blaze of orange and a mantle of purple. As it grew dark the stars came out.

Joe never moved. He was linked to the moving water and the feeding fish. To all of it.

The motel where they spent time together was located along the old highway west of the interstate a few miles south of Drew. Foxen was a bold man but he was also discreet. No rendezvous at the hotel on Main. Drew was a small town trying to grow itself big, but it was still small and that meant that everyone pretty well knew everyone and everyone's business—who was drinking too much, who was broke, who was beating who, and, number one on the list, who was screwing who. Well, Foxen, for largely subconscious reasons, had been screwing the Graves clan for decades, and wanted to keep at it. And he didn't need a bunch of northern high plains idiots up in arms and banded against him for violating some lame code of the West or whatever. All dark work benefited from stealth. He'd screwed Joe's father out of his land and coal, Joe out of his land and water and coal and way of life and out of what Joe liked to think of as his woman. Mickey. Yeah, dear sweet, sexy, and hard-as-nails Mickey. Foxen had met her during a preliminary meeting concerning mining the coal buried beneath the Workman Plateau. That was a few years back over at the Dark Star McCoy offices. A meeting of geologists, hydrologists, and biologists (hence Mickey), with a few attorneys thrown into the mix to make a thoroughly roguish gathering. Mickey did her bit there filling in the others on the curious ways of water in a parched land and its impact on the country. Now you see it and now you don't. Underground rivers and aquifers resembling subterranean lakes moved as if by magic through the porous layers of sandstone, limestone, and the rambling cracks between beds of clinker, shale, and, of course, coal. To count on tapping this water to put out what she termed even at this early stage, "fires from hell," water to douse the burning seams of coal at Yoter's and other locations on the plateau, to count on this water would be foolish, she said. And using this water may dry up the small creeks and springs on the plateau, creating havoc and devastation for both the flora and fauna up there. Other geologists and hydrologists slouched around the table ridiculed her assessments and opinions, saying that there was more than enough water to put out a thousand fires, and that the land would be fine regardless of the final state of the aquifer. There was plenty of water. Enough to last for centuries. Mickey stuck to her guns and closed with a vehement, "The bunch of you are not only assholes, you're also morons," and then she flashed each of the men and the one other woman in the room the most charming, subtly sexual smile Foxen had ever seen. After the meeting he called her aside and asked her to dinner and drinks. She accepted. She had always been drawn to older men. That dinner led to the first night at the motel south of town. The one with the hot pink and green neon trim that lit the eaves and flashed over and over ROCKIN R MOTEL. The one with the black-and-white TVs, no phones, and off-white chintz bedspreads. That was the first of many nights over the years, the frequency actually increasing after she started going with Joe. And given her ongoing relationships with both Foxen and Joe, Mickey was in a near constant state of intense sexual arousal. She glowed and burned like the coal on Elmer's land. Foxen knew about Joe, and he anticipated the day when he could stick it to Graves one more time, this time with the blatant knowledge that he was fucking Joe's woman. Why Foxen hated the Graveses even he didn't know. He'd thought on this often, and all of it came back to the fact that he only knew he wanted them to suffer and to see their lives destroyed. To feel otherwise would have meant casting his whole life, his reason for being, into doubt. Doubt was something Foxen never entertained. So he had flown up from Denver the next day like he told Kilduff he would. And he made it clear to Kilduff that nothing was going to stop Dark Star from getting the coal underneath the Workman, and Yoter's place in particular. The conglomerate never backed down. Money wasn't the issue. Power and the exercising of that power was what all this was about. Never show weakness or capitulation. Never. And the two men drank whiskey and smoked cigars to seal that fate. Foxen was intoxicated from wielding his power and Kilduff, against his best judgment, yielded. He had to choose between preserving his life and keeping his job. He chose his job. So Foxen screwed Mickey. Mickey screwed Joe. And Joe, Elmer, and the dogs howled at the moon.

"Joe knows about us," she said.

"Fuck him," he said.

The next morning Mickey pulled her pickup alongside an island at a gas station/supermarket in Drew and got out, as did her companion, Foxen. He pushed the appropriate button on one of the pumps, slid his credit card through the slot, and pushed more buttons before the machine said BEGIN PUMPING FUEL, which Mickey did. Unleaded supreme. Foxen went inside to grab a couple of packs of Newports for her. While the thirty-gallon tank swallowed the overpriced fuel, a steady, though tiny, stream of the stuff leaked onto the concrete. A hole the size of a twenty-penny nail had been poked through the pipe leading to the tank, perhaps from a strand of barbed wire or perhaps from a twenty-penny nail kicked up by the truck's tires while Mickey wheeled along the Workman's backroads. By the time Foxen returned, Mickey was putting the nozzle back in place at the pump. Neither of them noticed the puddle of gas beneath the truck. The station always smelled of gasoline, so nothing seemed unusual.

They both turned from looking at each other just as Joe drove up to another island of pumps some sixty feet away. He jumped out of the truck, pressed the PAY CASH INSIDE button, and began fueling his rig. He looked up just as Foxen returned to Mickey's truck. Foxen had seen Joe. Joe had seen him. Foxen put his arm around Mickey. She looked up at him and smiled. Then she saw Joe.

Foxen turned Mickey's head to face him and gave her a long kiss. Mickey made a weak attempt to pull away as she glanced at Joe, an expression of fear and confusion distorting her features.

Joe was at his limit with all of it—the haul road, the loss of his land because of the coal his father had sold, Mickey, Foxen—all of it. He looked at the .357 lying on the truck's bench seat, finished filling up the truck, replaced the hose, and went for his gun. He came around the back of his old truck with the pistol held slightly above waist level, just in time to see Foxen puffing on a cigar and lighting a smoke for Mickey with an Ohio Blue Tip stick match. Joe took aim at Mickey. Foxen, unaware of the pistol pointed at her, casually tossed the still-flaming match with a flick of his fingers. It arced, still burning, toward the ground and the pool of gas.

Joe leveled the gun's bead on her head and her eyes went wide with fear. He prepared to squeeze the trigger, taking time to consider whether he really wanted to kill someone he loved and whom he thought had loved him. He hated her, too, and seeing her with Foxen ripped at his insides. He wanted them both dead. Out of his life. Never to have existed. And he still loved her and knew he couldn't kill her. Killing Foxen meant nothing to him. Dead or alive this man was just one more shitty human to Joe. And Mickey, she was love to him and more pain in his life. Someone who gave a little of herself when it suited her purposes or satisfied her needs. Joe always fell for this, believing the little was the beginning of much more. It never was. The giving was nothing more than taking and he was tired of all of it. Alone was better. He could count on that. He thought this just as the gas ignited with a *whomp,* ripping away the fill pipe and setting off the fuel inside the truck's tank. Thirty gallons of high-octane gasoline ignited in a yellow-gold explosive roar that blew the rear end of the truck up and then the whole thing slowly turned over on its side. What Joe saw was Mickey's mouth saying *No. Please don't, Joe* and her body starting to slump toward the ground. Maybe from stress. Maybe she was fainting. Then she was shoved forward by the blast and simultaneously enveloped in burning gasoline. The explosion had slammed Joe against the tailgate and knocked him to the pavement. He heard Mickey scream, "Oh God! Joe help me." Not Foxen's name, but Joe's, and he knew then despite all of her meanness and selfishness that he had touched her somewhere inside and that in her own way, she loved him, too. Her hair blazed skyward in a flaming headdress. Foxen had time to form an embryonic look of stunned terror before he, too, was engulfed in flames. Joe watched as her burning body lurched to him in hideous, staggering steps then collapsed. Screams of agony, of pure intense pain, reached him. He could already smell the cooked flesh mixed with the odors of burning paint, tires, and fuel. The hair on Joe's arms and head was singed, as was his shirt. His skin felt like it had been burned.

All of this took place in seconds, but already he thought he could hear the wails of police, fire, and ambulance sirens. Mickey's and Joe's trucks had been the only vehicles at the station. He turned to his left and saw the attendant staring through a shattered window, the phone still held to his ear. Displays of cigarettes, lighters, and candy had been knocked all over the counter from the concussion of the blast. The kid's mouth hung open. Looking back, he saw a blackened form that was Mickey. Foxen's body was also charred black and bubbly, smoldering with more smoke than flame now. Her truck was burning steadily, especially the tires, which were billowing a thick, blue-black, greasy smoke.

Joe turned to the street and spotted two bright red fire trucks, lights flashing, pulling up to the simmering wreckage. A pair of white-and-orange ambulances were right behind, as was

Egyptian Healy in his cruiser followed by a Wyoming state patrol car. The scene was now filled with the deafening screams of sirens and strobing flashes of red, blue, white, and yellow flashing lights. Joe crawled to the cab of his truck and shoved the .357 under the seat amid a mess of crushed beer cans, brake fluid containers, wrenches, and lots of dirt and mud-caked weeds. He saw blood running down his cheeks and chin and soaking his shirt. He could feel something warm and sticky draining from his ears. Then he passed out, his head knocking against the rusty running board.

Rough weather on the Workman was nothing new. Wild storm fronts steaming up from the Gulf of Mexico, surging in from the Pacific, or wailing down from Alberta, brought severe wind, raging lightning, whiteout blizzards, cloudbursts, hail, sleet, intense heat, and numbing cold, year after year. Two feet of snow in May. Thunderstorms in January. One hundred twenty degrees in July. Sixty below in March. Or sixty above in February. None of this is uncommon on the Workman Plateau. The jet stream tracks directly across this country or oscillates just to the north or south.

Rough weather can look like a drought. The last week of September brought with it cloudless skies and temperatures in the midnineties. Record highs. The land was cooked to a dry, withered, golden brown. The softening light of autumn shone and flickered through the tall, dead grasses and now silvery sage with an unearthly intensity that flickered and played across the wind-polished surfaces of grass stems and seed heads, the radiance turning on and off, expanding and contracting at the whim of the warm breeze. In the mornings, the light dew glistened in the orange light of sunrise and looked like fields of highly polished diamonds, rubies, emeralds, and sapphires that had sprouted atop slender stalks of crystal, a vision offering prismatic magic that was at once spectacular to behold and blinding in its short-lived brilliance. But by midday, the indigo sky was cooked to a sun-blasted white, the intensity of the noon light washing out the landscape. Ponderosas, yucca, sage, buffalo grass, all looked like it was part of an overexposed photograph. The red, orange, ocher, lavender, and brown soils of the plateau held no moisture. The two-track and dirt roads that wound across and up and down the Workman, rising up through now dry coulees, up through parched stands of willow, alder, and large cottonwoods with their thick, rough gray bark and then finally drifting across the swales and flats of the plateau, those roads were covered with three, four, five inches of powdery dust that streamed behind a rancher's pickup like a wake behind a ship at sea. Devil winds whizzed and spun through the country, the whirling funnels now red, now brown, now shades of yellow, now a mixture of the the soils' colors.

The entire Workman appeared lifeless in this first week of fall. Antelope, mule deer, turkeys, hawks, rabbits, snakes, even the spiders and ants, along with almost every other creature living here, was either underground or hunkered down beneath the brush or overhanging rock outcroppings near dying springs. Cattle were dropping from thirst and hunger by the dozens everywhere, their pitiful bellowings rising hoarsely up from ponds now nothing more than cracked mudholes. The animals crowded together and pawed in vain at the hard ground. Angus and Hereford carcasses lay on their sides in the coulees and on the flats where the animals had looked for water, the desiccated hides stretched tight to ripping across thick ribs. Turkey vultures feasted and were the only ones that thrived in the blistering drought. Creeks were dried up, gone, nothing but dust-covered rocks and floury silt. Needles on the ponderosas were more gray than green. The layers of multicolored rock that made up the bluffs, buttes, and cliffs of the land, the exposed black seams of coal, the yellow, charcoal, and lime upthrusts of sandstone, the orange-brown chunks of clinker, all this rock and soil stood out in the heat beneath the dead sky in muted colors. The bizarrely eroded escarpments and pillars of stone looked as if they'd been lightly covered with white spray paint.

Spontaneous-combustion wildfires burned thousands of acres of the grassy flats and stands of pine, the fires only giving it up when they came to stretches of land that was nothing more now than dirt and rock. The air was often bitter with smoke until a hot afternoon wind blew the acrid stuff off toward South Dakota to the east. Then it smelled only of the hot sun and the overwhelming dryness. The seams of burning coal kept simmering, turning a hot landscape into a surreal furnace.

Mirages from the heat made the terrain look as though it were being viewed through cataracts as the country wavered and distorted in the baking air.

Life on the Workman had turned invisible. Rain and snow would bring the country back next year, but this season was over, finished. Precipitation was overdue and desperately needed to nourish the roots of all the plants that grew here, and the game that was dying of a desperate thirst.

Would the wet weather ever come, everyone asked. Would it come before the Workman was completely and absolutely reduced to ash and cinders?

In the long-term scheme of things these were foolish questions. Of course the storms would come with their billions of tons of moisture. Cactus, sage, ponderosa, coyote, mule deer, they'd all hang in there, more than likely in diminished numbers, but they'd come back when the Workman flowed again. The rain-laden clouds always returned and, as a matter of fact, a huge storm was building now, the kind that hits the Workman Plateau only every thousand years or so, a storm that would wash away the drought and a good deal more.

An enormous mass of warm, moist air was pulsing up from the Gulf. Uncommon but not unheard of for this time of year. And a Pacific system was slowly spinning like a miniature galaxy in the direction of the Sanders Mountains, the thick clouds riding in from the coast across Oregon and Washington. Lenticular clouds, curving brush strokes of moisture, were already arcing over the peaks of the Sanders, a sure sign of the harsh weather soon to come. To the north a dense mass of cold air was sweeping down from the Arctic, gathering still more moisture as it raced along the east slope of the Canadian Rockies. The eternal high pressure that had been locked over the Workman for weeks, the high that had been punishing the country for what seemed like forever to those who lived here, was about to be shoved east.

A storm was coming, but for now the land lay lifeless and baking in the heat.

Around noon a few weeks after the explosion at the gas station, Joe and Elmer were sitting on the hood of Elmer's truck sharing a bottle of Jim Beam rye, a semi-serious whiskey change of pace that brought a smile to the old man's suntanned and windburned face.

It was another hot day, but finally after many weeks there were clouds building over the Sanders Mountains and all along the western horizon. Perhaps some moisture was in sight.

"Haven't had a bottle of this shit in years, Joe," said Elmer, as he took a decent hit. "Damn good booze, though." He wiped his mouth on his shirtsleeve. "Whiskey, rye whiskey. Whiskey I cry. If I don't get rye whiskey. I surely must die. Yes indeed. Nothing like it."

"It goes down. That's all I ask." Joe winked at Elmer, who smiled in the recognition that his friend was healing up, coming back from his private hell of the past few months. "Haven't had any either in a bit. Not since I brought you that case when you helped me with the calving in 'ninety-three." Joe lit a Camel, took a drink from the bottle, and set it on the hood. "That was a bitch of a spring, Elmer. Snowed all of March, most of April, and then some more in May."

"Like that sometimes," said Elmer as he flicked pieces of bacon rind to the Boykins seated in their usual semicircle around the two men. He'd fried up several pounds of the tough meat the other day, the pork a gift from Coaker, who'd butchered a pair of his Landrace hogs. Tenderloins and two-inch-thick pork chops were also part of the package. Elmer would reciprocate the next time he cut up one of his Angus. He did have a couple of dozen Texas longhorns fattening up on some fenced acreage along some bottomland by the Dolphy River, but he could never bring himself to kill them, always saying that every time he looked at "their scrawny asses and long-beat-all-to-hell-pointed horns," he started feeling "all romantic with it all." When Joe heard that, he gave Elmer a good deal of static along lines of "Montana is where men are men and sheep are scared," modified with the longhorn variation. Elmer would just laugh it away and say that he'd gotten all he wanted when he was younger, and Joe would counter with "Sheep or steers?" and then Elmer would laugh again and say, "You're a twisted shit, Joe, old boy."

The two had been discussing the aftermath of the explosion at the gas station. The paramedics had taken Joe to the Drew hospital where he'd spent a couple of days with a concussion and some secondary burns along his arms and face. The police came, asked some questions. Joe's brief answers satisfied them, so they left. IVs, hospital food, and officious nurses drove him out of the place as soon as he was able to sit up and locate his clothes, at least what was left of them. Shirt and T-shirt had been delicately pulled from his burns and then discarded, so Joe checked himself out wearing jeans, boots, and a hospital gown. "Worn worse," he said to the nurse. After that he'd killed the ensuing days drinking more than usual, which meant a lot, fixing fence, dealing with his cattle, and dealing with Mickey's death. Her remains had been sent back to Wisconsin to be buried with the rest of her family at a small cemetery along Turtle Creek in the southern part of the state. The lack of a funeral and a wake to grieve her loss hadn't helped Joe. He'd spoken with Elmer some about how he felt and his friend would smile ruefully and say, "Stay with it. All you can do is keep pushing. Pain always goes away, at least enough so you can get on with whatever this damn life has for us poor bastards next." Joe would return home and sit next to his little spring-fed trout stream, burning up the hours watching the brown trout as they fed on the emerging caddis and even some small mayflies that buzzed near the water's surface and among the willows. The fish never stopped feeding. *Do they ever rest?* he wondered. *God! I'd sure like to. I'm beat.* He'd be up at all hours of the night brooding about his life and seeing nothing good in it. And he'd listen to John Coltrane, something Elmer gave him unmerciful grief about. "Jazz. Shit. Sounds like someone pulling the tail off one of my dogs with vise grips. That's nothin' but pure-as-shit simple noise, son. Listen to Hank or Conway or Ferlin. Now that's some serious damn music. Those boys could carry a tune." Joe would shrug and even smile at this and say, "Coltrane makes sense to me." With the help of Coltrane's rhythms he'd always make it through the interminable night and by sunrise he'd be ready to face another day, eventually even with a trace of optimism.

After a couple of weeks, Joe had put the memory of Mickey in a place where it didn't dominate his life. He was at the stage where he could go about his day-to-day routine without thinking of her constantly. When he did remember her now, it felt like he was thumbing through an old photo album. Memories, some painful, some happy, but nothing that sliced through him like a jagged knife blade. That part of it was mostly over, but for some time after her death, usually around three A.M., Joe would roll out of his sweat-soaked bed, pull on jeans and a shirt, and go to the kitchen, where he'd build a fire in the woodstove and turn on Coltrane and his tenor sax before starting in on the whiskey, chain-smoking his Camels, and calling up the image of her in his mind and the memories of all that had passed between them.

"Fucking Foxen," he'd say.

"Fucking women," he'd say.

He'd loved her, still did way down deep in his heart and gut, but her sleeping with that bastard, a man who'd taken advantage of Joe and his father for decades, that thought, that horrible image would never go away and it would always darken his thoughts of her. He hated her. He always would. And he loved her. He always would. He was tired and sick of all of the pain that had shaped his life. He just wanted to live, to be left alone with some semblance of peace. "Run out the goddamn string," he'd mutter. And he'd say after he was very drunk, hand raised toward the eternal night sky out there above the kitchen ceiling, hand raised, middle finger extended, he'd say "The hell with you, God. The hell with you," and he'd think with a grim smile sliding across his face, *The hell with hell. I'm already there.* Then he'd see Mickey's face and bare breasts leaning over him the day they'd found the bison skull.

But even this misery was fading from his life. The sun kept burning up over the eastern edge of the plateau each morning and Joe did keep going, finding pleasure in the hard work of ranching. All he wanted now was to slide through the days without any additional pain. The whiskey had helped some, but not much, and he began to ease off the stuff. Instead, when the bottle beckoned, he'd walk the ravines and sage flats with his old banged-up Remington 870 Wingmaster, a gun his father had given him when he was eleven. He'd dropped a lot of birds with that gun. Sage grouse, sharptails, huns, chukar, pheasants, even turkeys. There were plenty of birds this year, and Joe had little trouble kicking up bunches of sharps as he pushed up brushy draws. Twenty, thirty, forty of the birds would explode from the brush in a whirring, clucking dusky-colored cloud of beating wings. And he'd raise the gun to his shoulder, automatically swinging through one of the grouse, both eyes open, pull the trigger, and then swing on another and shoot again. He did this so quickly, he often had time to see both birds tumble into the dry grass in soft heaps and watch as tufts of feathers drifted down through the lifeless air. Then he'd walk up the rest of the now scattered grouse and shoot some more. He'd do this every afternoon right when the sun began dropping down to the western mountains. He'd walk and flush the sharptails and shoot half a dozen or so and then he'd wander the flats working up a six-or-seven-pound sage hen or two. He'd get on them quickly, before they had time to work their wings to maximum thrust and power away from him in seconds. Most people didn't like the strong, gamy taste of these birds, but Joe did. He'd soak them in milk for hours, rinse them, then marinate them in a mixture of white wine, olive oil, bay leaf, rosemary, lots of garlic, salt, freshly ground pepper, and a bunch of sliced lemons. Then he'd grill them over a hot fire, constantly basting the browning flesh with the marinade. A green salad and the grouse, some sharpies, too, and maybe a bottle of the Merlot, and then he'd go out on the porch and sip some whiskey and smoke his Camels well into the dark, star-packed night. That's how he lived now. Ranch work. Shooting birds. Drinking some, smoking and thinking, and sometimes talking with Elmer. He was finding out about inner quiet and peace for the first time in his life and the stillness within him was at once frightening, lonely, and powerful. The strength and serenity of isolation and calm were making his life bearable and moving him farther in distant directions, territory where he was completely alone with his thoughts but at the same time completely aware of others wandering the same wavelengths. Voices would come to his internal conversations and talk with him like old friends do around a nighttime fire with a shared bottle. All of them sounding different but all of them familiar in unremembered ways. Like seeing a river somewhere for the first time and recognizing that the riffles, pools, and brushy banks were a lot like his miniature trout stream. The voices were like that. Nothing outrageously revelatory. Just talk in his head with those he'd never met, but had always known. "You're completely nuts, Joe," he'd say out loud and he'd laugh and the voices would say, *We all are. Who cares?* And he grew used to his new way of hearing things and he never said a word about this to Elmer, but one night the old guy looked at him with a glint in his eyes and said, "Crazy as all hell are the voices we listen to, but it beats the good goddamn hell out of pretending we don't hear them, don't it, Joe," and before he could reply, Elmer was off by the back porch feeding the sixteen Boykins, and Joe just looked at all of them and up at the sky and inside himself and said softly, "Damn right, Elmer."

After Foxen was killed his remains were shipped back to Denver in a company jet, cremated—a redundant touch, Joe thought—and buried in some cemetery near Arvada. He'd purchased a plot there amid the condos and high-rises that had once been sage hills and flats. Kilduff convinced the Dark Star board to pull off of the Workman and stick with the McCoy mine, work that land over until it played out in another ten or fifteen years. Then the Consortium would move on to another part of the planet and start all over with the scraping, blasting, and digging. For now, at least, the Workman Plateau was spared, and so was Joe's place. The haul road was still in, but Dark Star had graded it over and scattered some wild grass seed on the dirt, the thin kernels lying on the soil baking under the sun or blowing away in the dust with the onset of the predictable hot afternoon wind. The water-pumping gear had been hauled away a few weeks back. Huge trucks carried the skeletonlike drilling structure, the large pumping equipment, and all the piping back to McCoy. As for the new rail line, that was on hold. The one already at Decker could handle that mine's coal output. The river had been spared, too, for a few years, anyway. It was already washing away much of the damage done by the construction. Rock, gravel, and oil-soaked soil were sucked up by the patient river's current and carried downstream toward the Yellowstone River, a hundred or more miles to the north. Maybe the material would eventually find its way to the Gulf of Mexico. At least St. Louis. The environmentalists proclaimed Dark Star's pullout on the Workman as a "victory for the earth and our environmental crusade." So they went off to fight their holy war somewhere else. Something about slaughtered bison or maybe it was the grizzlies up along the Swan Crest in north-western Montana.

For the first few days after the explosion, the conversation in Drew and among area ranchers was dominated by the fiery deaths of Mickey and Foxen, and the fact that the disaster took place right in front of Joe's eyes; that part, right in front of his eyes, was a big selling point. The horror of watching other humans burn to death in unimaginable agony worked its perverse magic on people's minds for many hours and across the distorted insights of countless drinks. But for them, as for people everywhere, after pounding the subject matter over from all angles at least ten thousand times, the story grew old, especially when news broke that Wyoming's governor had been discovered by his wife's private investigator in a Cheyenne motel room with two fourteen-year-old boys. That one would play for a month or so anyway. Perversion in its varied forms always pulled at people's minds. "Never get enough of that shit," Elmer said.

Life went on all along the Workman. Joe's physical wounds healed with some scarring. His emotional injuries knitted, also, but with some scar tissue of their own, and life did indeed roll on. And Joe found himself at Elmer's this morning with the rye whiskey and he even felt happy for the first time in many long weeks. Elmer noticed the change in attitude. He clapped him on the shoulder and said, "Not bad half-ass shape for a spineless dipshit like yourself. Beginnin' to think you're gonna make it. God help us all." Then he led Joe to the hood of the old truck. The spaniels were already there waiting for them. Way ahead of the game as usual.

Joe looked over his shoulder to the west and south and saw two distinct lines of purple-black clouds advancing on the Workman. Both fronts were towering, dense walls. The leading edges were spinning and boiling and sending small vertical tornadic spikes down to the ground. He could see, even from this distance, the thick curtains of precipitation sweeping the mountains and foothills. Lightning strikes were arcing up from the ground into the storms, and the muffled sound of distant thunder rumbled across the Workman.

"Damn nasty weather coming, Elmer. I knew it when I saw the lenticulars yesterday. Those clouds always mean weather. Heat's gonna break soon."

"Up north doesn't look too damn inviting either." Both men examined a similar storm mass bearing down from up Alberta way. The temperature was now dropping toward eighty, down from a noontime reading of a record ninety-six in the shade, according to Elmer's large, clocklike thermometer nailed to a beam on the front porch. A cool gust of wind out of the west kicked up some red-brown dust, ruffled the dogs' curly hair, and blew Joe's old, beat-up Chicago Cubs hat off his head and toward the sage flat in the east. "And holy shit, Joe. Lookit over cast. There's more goddamn weather building out there. Kee-rist, must be a damn hurricane or something. Damn storms are coming at us from all directions. We're surrounded. Pass the goddamn whiskey."

Another blast of wind, this one smelling of cold rain and shooting up from the south, knocked over a shovel and rake over by the stockyard.

"We're in for it, buddy," said Elmer around a slug of rye. "I can sense it. This one's gonna blow everything to kingdom come. Maybe even put out those fires." He pointed in the direction of the hole in the ground, the one that had swallowed a Dark Star truck and two of its men, the place where the explosion had torn the earth wide open. Smoke was still issuing from the tear in the land, and the ground for hundreds of yards all around the blast site was too hot to walk on. "Yes sirree, I think my barbecue is about to be put on goddamn permanent hold real damn soon."

"I've never seen anything like this around here," said Joe, as he stubbed out his smoke, lit another, and reached for the whiskey. "Bad weather from a couple of directions, sure, but never coming in on us from all over the place. This shit's coming in fast and from everywhere."

Before Elmer could answer, gusts of cold air whipped down on them from each side, forming a miniature tornado out on the edge of the sizzling sage flat. The funnel drove straight for a metal grain bin that expanded then imploded with the rapidly fluctuating air pressure caused by the tightly spinning air. Then the corrugated structure enlarged like a balloon and ripped apart. Thousands of kernels of dried corn were sucked into the air like a gigantic swarm of bees. From there the mini tornado rocked off toward Elmer's barn and flattened half of that before bouncing and buffeting out across the prairie headed east, shooting small bolts of static electricity over in odd directions, each strike sounding like the report of a high-powered rifle. Sage bushes, roots and all, were sucked out of the ground and whirled to the top of the now full-scale tornado.

Even from a distance of a quarter mile or so the shriek of the tormented air sounded like someone was grinding an enormous ax blade on a stone wheel. A sage bush was ejected from the cyclone, and the six-foot plant shot straight at Joe and Elmer, who both dived to the ground an instant before the bush smashed through the truck's window. That sent the sixteen Boykins scurrying to the front porch, umber eyes wide with excitement, thirty-two ears flapping in the wind.

Elmer stood up clutching the unspilled whiskey and yelled, "Damn storm's gonna son-of-a-bitchin' level my place," and took a huge pull of the rye. "Tell you what I'm thinking, Joe. I hope every damn thing gets flattened in this rigmarole," he bellowed. "Time to build some new structure around here. Build a big goddamn tower for the telescope and really give those heavens a once-over. Give me something to do. Idle hands are the work of the devil. Know what I mean 'bout that there shit?"

"Elmer, you're crazy as hell," roared Joe above the wind that was now hammering the land from all directions at steadily increasing beat. Fifty-, sixty-, seventy-mile-an-hour gusts. And lightning strikes crashing all around them every second. The storm's velocity and volume hurt their ears. The temperature was in the forties now, a fifty-degree drop in twenty minutes. High-altitude cirrus clouds muted the sun before they were in turn blocked out by walls of cumulonimbus. Mean-looking clouds like large breasts quickly formed beneath the base of the wall, pulsed to the ground and then back into the dark heart of the storm. All four fronts were now within a few miles of Elmer's place. Gulf of Mexico, Pacific, Arctic, and eastern Montanan. Then it grew darker and started to hail. Small, pea-sized stones that quickly grew to the size of golf balls and covered the ground in white. The hail clanged off the trucks and metal outbuildings and banged on top of the remains of the wooden barn and smashed out the remaining windows in Elmer's home, the ones not boarded up from the coal seam explosion a while back. When the glass shattered, the shards cascaded down on the porch and the ground or were sucked by the wind out onto the plateau.

"Elmer, I'm going back to my place to ride this out," screamed Joe as a hailstone bounced off his head. "I'll cut back along the edge of your inferno. It'll save time."

"You'll never make it, but give 'er hell for me." Elmer lurched off to the shelter of the porch to join his dogs, all sitting along the wall of the house well out of the line of fire. Several chunks of ice, now the size of tennis balls, slammed into his back and shoulders, but he kept going and made the porch, swearing a blue streak all the way. Joe tore open the door to his truck, fired up the engine, and shifted gears, as hailstones the size of grapefruits took out his windshield. He drove off with a lap full of smashed pieces of glass the shape of huge diamonds and a pair of rock-hard snowballs bouncing around. In the rearview mirror he saw Elmer laughing and talking to the Boykins, and then, with the bottle of Beam in his hand, he saw his friend pointing at something to the north, off in the direction of Joe's place. The rain came in sheets, a downpour, and that was the last he saw of Elmer. The storm dominated everything now. All he could see in front of him was the hood of the truck and a few feet of muddy ruts. He drove on like a madman, trusting in his familiarity with the roads to see him through.

The speedometer in the old truck said he was doing fifty. Maybe he was. More likely the wheels were spinning through the muck, melting hail, and pooling rainwater. The steering wheel bucked and lurched in his hands as the front end bounced through deep ruts and across fresh washouts in the red mud that used to be the road running from Elmer's along the ruined sage flat then down into Mad Woman Gulch and up again to Joe's place. He couldn't see ten feet in front of him. The rain was coming down in a wall of water. Rips of lightning illuminated the land around him, turning the countryside into a quick-flashing series of monotone still-life images. Fleeing antelope caught in full stride. A golden eagle frozen in flight. Swaying pines stooped at odd angles to the ground.

A white-hot bolt hammered a lone juniper on the edge of the road. The small tree exploded in a cloud of blasted wood and smoke. Joe instinctively swerved to avoid the strike, running over a small upthrust of clinker just off the road as the lightning exploded with a deafening crash. The front end of the truck kicked into the air and then its momentum pushed the rig off into the sage, the truck flying through space and listing toward the passenger side. Joe clung to the wheel and braced for the impact as the truck slammed to the ground fifty feet from the road. The Ford slid on its side, grinding against rock and pushing into the saturated soil. Pieces of sagebrush, entire plants flew into the cab. All of this happened in seconds, but Joe felt as though he were watching everything in exceptionally slow motion. He watched while hanging on to the wheel with clenched fists as the truck plowed into rocks, pieces of grillwork and shattered headlights flying up over his side of the cab. Sounds of tearing metal, fragmenting glass, and shearing chrome trim reached his ears above the storm's din. A spray of mud and small rock poured through the space where the windshield used to be. A splintered piece of sage embedded itself in his upper arm and his face felt like it was being mangled by shotgun pellets.

The truck finally stopped sliding. The rain and lightning were stronger than ever. The wind was howling, moaning like an insane beast. He could smell the steam from the truck's ruined radiator and the odor of leaking gasoline. The door on his side was crumpled shut, but the window on the driver's side was smashed out and Joe worked his way through the opening, shoving branches of sage out of the way. He worked his chest free, then wriggled his legs clear, falling to the mud with a wet thump. He pulled the stick from his arm and blood poured out. He tried to stand up but the wind slammed him against the drivetrain of the exposed undercarriage, knocking him back down. He crawled around to the front of the truck but there was no relief from the wind and rain. A series of lightning strikes to his right illuminated the tear in the earth caused by the burning coal seams. Enormous jets of steam and fountains of orange-red sparks were exploding all along the huge rip in the plateau. The wind dropped for an instant and now he could hear the roar of the vaporizing rainfall, the bursting sound of the seams of coal that were at once exploding into sheets of fire and also being extinguished by the downpour that was like no rain Joe had ever seen in his life. Not rain, rather an avalanche of water now along with the constant flash and afterglow of lightning and the fusillade of roaring thunderclaps.

The wind picked up where it had left off and increased in intensity. Sagebrush, ponderosa limbs, hunks of grass, whole juniper trees, rocks blew past him in all directions as the gale swirled and ravaged the land. A tremendous gust blew the truck on its back, collapsing the cab roof; then another shrieking blast rolled the pickup in the direction of the steaming inferno. Joe was blown against a small rise of limestone, the force of the impact breaking his right arm and tearing a gash in his leg. He wrapped his arms and legs around a rectangular piece of the rock and screamed, "Go ahead you bastard. Kill me. KILL ME!" and he saw through the rain and the blood his truck roll over and over, wheels flying from the axles, frame contorting, the Ford rolling to the edge of the widening crevasse and then disappearing. Seconds later the gas tank exploded. A ball of flame rose briefly above the rim of the gash before the rain beat down the flames.

"I'm a dead man," he yelled, and thought about Elmer telling him to "give 'er hell." He renewed his grip on the rock as the wind roared around him. The air grew colder.

He held this way for eternity, becoming part of the gritty stone, until he noticed that the gale was letting up some. So was the rain. The lightning and thunder were moving off to the east and now the temperature was below freezing. He was cold and he thought, *That's something. Cold means I'm still alive.* The rain stopped and the wind died. He let loose of the rock, rolled away in the hardening mud. He slowly stood up and moaned when he felt the broken bone. He looked around and all he could see was the nearby sage flat swept clean of all plants and trees. The earth had been scoured to a lifeless, barren landscape. The storm had sucked water from the small ponds and little creeks. He could see the funnels of steam rising from the rent in the ground but no more flames or sparks. The land was dead still. Dark purple and black clouds swirled and boiled soundlessly only a few hundred feet above him. It was now so cold that the puddles of water had ice on their edges and the mud was almost hard. The hard taste of snow tinged the air. All was silent except for the distant-sounding hiss of steam.

WAHHHOOOARRERRR . . .

The sound tore across the land and through Joe. He looked over to where the flat dropped into Mad Woman Gulch.

The wolf was standing there staring at him. Huge. Four hundred pounds. Nearly four feet tall at the shoulder. Massive head. Jaws filled with huge, menacing teeth that glistened bone-white. Deep yellow eyes glowed in the dim light. The animal moved several paces nearer him and roared again.

WAHHHOOOARRERRR . . .

The howl froze Joe. A sound from another time. Wild. Primitive. Ancient.

The wolf stood motionless and the two creatures, man and wolf, looked at each other over the distance of time. The wolf's eyes glowed even more brightly and beams of light from the animal's soul seemed to burn into Joe. All he could see was a brilliant band of white light like an electric river flowing from his mind to join the larger current that was the wolf. The streams merged and Joe ceased being Joe. He was the wolf killing the mastiffs then loping across the high plains in the night. He was his father watching the enormous cat leaping over him in that Sierra Madre Occidental canyon so long ago. He was Mickey screwing Foxen. He was Elmer hopping up and down smoking a cigar and drinking the rye whiskey as he and the sixteen Boykins cavorted around the storm-leveled remains of his ranch house. He was all of those at Wimp's funeral alongside the road decades ago and he smelled the antelope cooking and sizzling over the fire and he heard Coaker playing his fiddle and everyone laughing. And then he was the Workman. He flowed through the river canyon and up his little stream. He was liquid and he was the layers of coal, slate, and sandstone. He saw the forever vastness of the plateau from the high limbs of ponderosa. He felt the wind stream through the trees' long needles. And he watched as countless rattlesnakes and milk snakes and gopher snakes poured from openings in the piles of sandstone and from holes in the ground beneath the sage plants. And he smelled the pungent sweetness of those plants. The hiss and rattle of the snakes became him. The rock, the animals, the subterranean rivers flowing beneath the forest of ponderosas and the barren sage flats, he was all of this and the wind sailing through everywhere, and he saw far beyond Mad Woman Gulch to the view from the summit of Chambers Point. He saw the solid land flowing eternally with its own rhythms, flowing through eons, rising and falling and re-forming again, and he watched forests come and go, and rock cliffs carved by the wind crumble to stone and dust, and he watched a land that was glowing simultaneously under a radiant sun and a star-packed night sky, and a huge moon perpetually rose and fell pouring silver light over the Workman. The northern lights. Meteors. Saint Elmo's fire. He watched all of this over time because he was the land and he saw the wolf looking into him and saying with a voice that knew no language, *All of this. All of us. One. The land.* And he stepped through the writhing and coiling rings of snakes and walked toward the edge of the cliff on the northern edge of Chambers Point where he watched Jupiter, a gigantic, swirling mass of colorful gases rising above the bluffs. And now he walked through a million years of the softly falling snow and stepped off the cliff trusting in the river of blue-white light . . .